AREION
FURY MC

CALIX

CALIX

BOOK SIX

AREION FURY MC SERIES

ESTHER E. SCHMIDT

Cover design by:

Esther E. Schmidt

Proofreader:

Christi Durbin

Editor:

Virginia Tesi Carey

Model:

Mike Minervini

@MrFitnessBoston

Photographer:

Reggie Deanching

www.rplusmphoto.com

DEDICATION

Christi. We share a brain and so much more.
One soul, two bodies and all that shit isn't just for
romance, it's what friendship is all about too.
Proud to have you as my best freaking friend out there.
We started this journey together when I wrote the first
book in this series. You've touched every single book
I wrote. Now, with closing this series…all these years
later…you still make me laugh at the moments I need
it the most, smack my head and ass when needed,
and listen when my heart is full. It's an honor to return
the favor any time of day, because having a friend
like you is the most precious of gifts this life can give.

Thanks, babe,
I Fucking love you!

CHAPTER ONE

CALIX

Leaning back, I cross my arms in front of my bare chest and glance around the dimly lit room. It's busy for a Thursday night, but it's the third Thursday of the month and that's the day members are allowed to bring a non-member. Kinda like an introduction night but with rules set in place. They have to be familiar with the BDSM scene, otherwise they need to take the training class first.

There are sounds of pleasure flowing through the air along with slaps, skin on skin action, growls, and sharp commands. Everyone around is busy with their own scene, leaving the bar empty. Hence the reason I can take a moment to relax. This place used to give me some kind of comfort. Watching, teaching, doing the occasional scene on stage, yet nothing about this appeals to me anymore.

Glancing down, I debate putting my cut back on. I stashed it on a shelf underneath the bar when Otis asked me to show off my abs. Normally I wouldn't even give anyone a moment of consideration if they'd asked me that question, but I was feeling generous and Otis wanted to teach the sub he picked for the night a lesson. Openly gawking at another Dom isn't a smart move for a sub. Therefore he needed to educate her; she won't be making that mistake again any time soon.

Besides...Otis is a good friend of mine who I've only recently made a partner. I deliberately made myself a silent partner so I can step away from the club for as long as I want or need to for that matter. This will be my last night in here for a while. I need it. Time for myself to figure out what I want to do. I've had too many damn jobs. Next to owning and running this club, I was a police detective and a bartender at the Purple Bean a few nights per week.

The Purple Bean is a bar owned by the Areion Fury

MC. Oh yeah, I'm also a biker if the mention of my leather cut didn't make it clear yet. Though I only wear my cut inside the club. Outside? Detectives need to dress the part and wearing suits was something I always did. With a preference to serene white ones in particular. Except I recently turned in my badge.

Everything's lost its appeal for some fucked up reason and I feel like I've lost my grip on things. Hence the reason I've stepped back from everything. My brain is always working, nothing new there, that's why I have…or had, so many jobs. I also have the personal obligation to visit my parents next week, so my ass will be on a plane for a mini vacation in London. After that? The hell if I know what I'll do.

The door connected to the hallway opens. Behind it exists a small entry room where people have to sign in to get inside the club. Esmee, the one who staffs the desk on Thursdays and Fridays, strolls inside and behind her follow two women. All I can make out is that one's a brunette and the other one is a blonde.

Esmee looks back at the women. "Please sit down, I'll be right back." She turns her attention to me. "Sir, could you please get them something to drink? I have to search for Master Mike to double check some-thing."

"Very well, Esmee." I push myself off the counter I was leaning against and stroll over as Esmee dashes away from the bar, heading for the dungeon in search of Mike.

"Ladies, there's a one drink rule, so if you intend to play you can have one now or after. Otherwise it's bot-tled water, tea, or coffee," I tell the two women whose faces I haven't seen yet. The both of them simply ig-nore me.

"I can't believe I let you talk me into bringing you along with me," the brunette whispers to the blonde.

The blonde leans forward. "It's not like I have a choice. My dad said this was our only shot so,"

"Ladies," I snap. "It's rude to ignore someone who's speaking to you and offering you a drink."

The blonde slowly turns and when our eyes connect it feels like I'm touching a live wire. Damn. Where everything in life was dull and plain a moment ago, suddenly something spectacular rises within my reach. It's rare for my body to react in such a way, even more when it's because of a woman.

Even with the dim light I can easily see the tiny scar on her chin. I can't tell what shade her eyes are and that somehow nags me, yet they are striking no matter the color they would be. It seems like she has syrup sweet lips, and I make a mental note to find out soon. High cheekbones, strong jaw, she's elegant, yet…bubbly? I don't think I've ever described a woman as bubbly.

Damn that long neck, leading to a stunning bosom that is strapped tight in a leather corset. I'm feeling so off my game for a moment that my fingers are digging into the wood of the bar. I haven't done a scene in here in a while, not to mention I haven't had sex in a very long time…but I want it all, and I want it right fucking now. But all of this aside? I'm the one being rude now, and that never fucking happens. I'm still openly gawking at this beauty in front of me.

The woman is about to say something when the door to the hallway bursts open and two guys step inside. They are both wearing Areion Fury MC cuts but I don't recognize either of them. Glancing down I notice the Ohio patch. The big one looks somewhat familiar now that I take a second look and yet I can't remember why or how.

I'm glad Esmee wasn't in her seat because I doubt she could have stopped these two from getting inside the club. Otis stalks toward them. "Gentlemen. Can I help you?"

"No. Ah, there she is. This will only take a moment, then we'll be gone." The big one steps around Otis and gets in the face of the blonde. "Did you really think you could find some kind of miracle worker in here? One who would stand a chance against me? Stupid cunt. Don't you realize that there's nothing you can do? Your father will blow out his last breath soon and then,"

The blonde punches the fucker straight in the eye and makes him stumble back, not expecting her outburst. I've seen enough. Why can't people ever be civil? I grab my cut, pull it on and jump over the bar. I'm just in time to intervene with the idiot who wants to lay a hand on a woman.

Grabbing his fist midair, I snap, "You don't have any authority to do business here. Obviously, you are no longer welcome. I suggest you take your brother along with you and leave."

The big one eyes my cut and suddenly, standing

this close, I can place the fucker. Dane Gilton. I fought this one a few times in underground fighting matches over a decade ago. He always lost but never gave up and kept challenging me. I hope he wants to have another fight because my hands itch to get a few punches in. I've been craving a chance to blow off some steam.

"Well, well, well. Who do we have here? Calix. Man, I thought you fell off the face of the earth ten years ago, but it seems you've just been hiding in this stinkhole, huh?" Dane chuckles.

I have to take a deep breath because I'm anything but calm right now and I never lose my shit. I've been brought up learning to control my temper, and I'm not going to start losing it right now in the middle of my own damn club, and we're drawing a crowd as it is.

"Leave," I snap.

"Not without Tenley," he barks back.

Tenley? "Who?"

There's a hand sliding over my shoulder as I feel a hot breath stroking my ear. "You're *the* Calix?"

She empathizes 'the' as if I've got a reputation. If she knows this idiot in front of me, she might know

I've done my fair share of underground fighting where I had a reputation that made a lot of people envy me. I don't look back but keep my gaze on the threat, Dane, and give her a grunt as an answer instead.

"Big Oaks is asking for a favor. He said if anyone could help me, it would be you." Her whispered words might mean nothing to anyone but for me? Fuck.

Big Oaks, President of Areion Fury MC, Ohio Chapter, and also a man I felt was more a father to me than my own ever was. Big Oaks was my trainer when I started underground fighting. The week I would have become his VP, I got transferred with a job offer as a detective I couldn't pass up. Big Oaks understood and wanted me to take the opportunity and called in a favor Zack owed him. That's how I ended up here, with Zack as my president.

"You know damn sure there's no other way around this, Tenley. Hiding behind Calix here won't do any good either. He's not a part of our chapter." Dane sneers.

"Last and final warning before I call it in. I'm sure my Prez would love to hear a biker from another chapter is pissing on his turf." My voice is matter-of-fact.

On the inside I'm fuming and ready to punch this guy's lights out like I did so many times in the past.

He eyes me and realizes his mistake. Tenley gets a deadly glare before he seethes, "This ain't over VP." He's out the door, taking his brother with him.

I double check my pecs and although I know damn well I'm not wearing a VP badge, but that would mean...no, that's not possible. Spinning around, I lock eyes with Tenley, the fucking gorgeous woman. "You're his VP?" I ask stunned. "Fucking A. Ohio's got a woman as a VP? How's that even possible?"

Her delicate finger with a long nail that's all shiny with lilac nail polish pokes into my leather cut. "Yes. I'm the VP. Do you have the same mindset as those bozos who just left? Think I'm incapable of my tasks because I don't have a cock between my legs? Because I can tell you right now, I do have the balls." Her hands cup her damn bosom and give them a squeeze.

Shit. I think my cock just jumped a few inches inside my leathers, cheering for the size of her balls. Again, my insides don't match my outside when I calmly say, "That's a count of ten for mouthing off."

Her well-groomed eyebrow raises. "A count of...

what?" she squeaks.

"Tenley, what the hell did I tell you before we got here? Shut up and put your head down. He's a Dom, you're in his BDSM club. Quit while you're ahead, girl," the brunette mutters to her friend.

All the while she's still glaring at me, so now I'm the one raising an eyebrow, and fuck…this is the first time in months I actually love the fact that I'm a Dom and have a very nice sub standing in front of me that is due a count of ten by my hand.

"I don't belong to you or to this club, I just came in to find you." Her eyebrows go down, clearly not understanding what she's in for.

"Well, congratulations, you found me," I tell her and grab her upper arm to spin her around and head for one of the private chambers. "Otis, take over bar duty."

I don't even hear my friend's reply and to be honest, I don't care. Taking the first available room on the right, I guide her in and close the door behind me, activating the red lightbulb next to the door on the outside to make others aware the room is occupied.

She turns around to face me and starts, "Listen."

"No," I snap. "You listen. I'm going to ask you

three questions. Depending on the answers, I will decide what happens next. There's only one other option…and that's throwing you out on your delicate ass right now. You got me?"

She doesn't say anything, but that upper lip of hers is twitching with anger and those brilliant eyes I now notice are blue flames with a healthy dose of temperament are making my cock twitch. Dammit. Why did I bring her here to have a talk when this room is designed for a scene, one I'm sure would create fireworks between us?

"First question. How do you know Big Oaks?"

Her features soften a bit before I can see her putting a hard mask in place. "He's my Prez."

I get the sense she's not telling me everything but I can tell she answered truthfully. "Second, why does he think I could help you?"

"Because he said the only one who could beat Dane Gilton at his own game was you." Her hands clench, making those lilac fingernails press into her skin as she places her tiny fists on those damn lush hips of hers.

"Third. And remember, be civil. It's just a question." I wait for her to give me a nod before I ask,

"How come you're the VP of the Ohio chapter? A woman isn't allowed that kind of title. Hell, a woman isn't even allowed in church."

"It might be unheard of but times change. And besides, I worked hard for it. I took the same road everyone else took and earned it. But it's also my right," she tells me in a defensive tone before her voice tinges with a hint of worry. "And with that, it should also be my birthright to become Prez when my father dies. If I was a guy, there would be no question about it. Except Dane Gilton thought if I was his ol'lady, he would become Prez automatically. Not to mention the fact that he would like to help my dad draw his last breath so he can claim me by force and take that gavel himself."

"I see." Leaning back against the wall, I let all of this work over in my head.

"That's all you've got to say?" she practically snarls.

"Didn't I tell you to be civil?" I raise my eyebrow and yet she doesn't even back down or anything. Nope, she narrows her eyes at me.

I don't think I've had a chick stand up to me like this, and fuck...that does fuel the lust that's burning inside me already.

"Did you sign the papers at the front door? The ones Esmee gave you?" And I might just feel my heart pause to wait for her reply.

"Yes," she snaps, all damn innocent as to why I'm asking that pesky little detail.

"Good." Fuck yeah. My heart kicks back in and my hands start to itch. "See that bench over there? That's called a spanking bench. That's where I want you. That tight black, latex skirt you're wearing needs to be tugged up over your hips. Present me that ass so you can take your punishment."

Her eyes go wide and she begins to sputter.

"Relax. You owe me a count of fifteen. That's how many times my hand will touch your ass. Nothing more, nothing less. You've signed an agreement to follow the rules of the club, you've misbehaved twice. And if there's anything you want my help for, I would advise you to settle this between us first." I've not moved one muscle and yet her breathing is rapid and so is her eye movement.

She's bouncing her gaze between the spanking bench and me. "You can't…it's not…I've not done anything like this."

"Ah, your first time, well…normally I would advise you to take the training class, but it's a little late for that." I can't help but smirk. "You're lucky, you know…this was my last night here at the club."

"Jeezzz, yeah, lucky me for getting my ass spanked by the only one who can save my club. Now that sounds promising," the woman mutters.

"Hey." I make sure to harden my voice. "I haven't decided if I would help you…yet. But presenting that ass of yours and taking your punishment would make a good start."

I only have time to blink once before she launches herself at me. I manage to dodge her fist, grab that wrist and spin her around so her back is pressing against my front. I've got both her hands in one of mine and with my free hand I grab her by that thick, long blonde hair and now realize that underneath, near her scalp, it's lilac. Fuck, that's fitting to her fierce yet bubbly attitude.

"You want my help?" I growl.

"Yes," she growls right back at me.

"I have two conditions. Non-negotiable ones," I state and tug the blonde and lilac silk that's running through my fingers.

Her damn eyes dilate as her gaze slides to my lips. "Deal," she breathes, not even questioning what the two conditions are.

"Good answer," I tell her before I slam my mouth down over hers.

CHAPTER TWO

TENLEY

Sweet heaven above, now *this* is kissing. But it's also very dangerous. This man has a hold on me with one arm, a tight grip on both my wrists while his fist is in my hair guiding my head. He's dominating me, consuming me, surrounding me in a world that revolves around him. And I damn well revel in it.

The sting on my scalp, the way his tongue slides against and around mine is making my whole body tingle. *I want him.* Badly. Doesn't even matter that I don't have a clue who he is or that I have to bend over that bench he pointed out so he can spank my ass…because that's what he said the count of fifteen will entail.

As long as he's the one in charge...I'm ready to follow every command. Shit.

That right there makes me bite his bottom lip. I can't throw myself at a guy like I did in the past. That will only turn around and blow up right in my face. His growl, and the fury that's blasting through his eyes, is the only indication that I've angered him. The rest of this captivating man is the serene coolness he's had in place the whole time I've seen him.

"First condition, whatever I say goes." His dark chocolate voice rumbles over my face.

Dammit. I already agreed when he hotwired my body, overriding my brain in the process when he was holding me like that. I don't have a choice since I need his help. That leaves me to nod while fuming on the inside. I must not hide it as well as he does because the corner of his mouth twitches.

"And the second one is?" I question because I do learn from my mistakes. I was stupid enough not to ask a moment ago so this might save me from surprises in the future.

"You'll hear it soon enough. The first one is all you need to know for now." His gaze goes to my lips and right when I think he's going to kiss me again, he releases his grip and steps back.

Shit. I actually stumble and catch myself in time not to fall on my ass. Calix is just standing there, watching me until his eyes go over my shoulder and back to me. Double shit. The spanking bench. I was kinda hoping he'd skip that part.

Okay, I need to get a grip on this situation. "Thank you for agreeing to help. Maybe you could meet with,"

"I gave you an order earlier. Present me your ass so we can deal with your punishment and have a little chat afterward." His voice doesn't leave any room for disagreement.

His whole demeanor doesn't as a matter of fact. My father's right…if there's anyone who can handle Dane, it's this man right here. Because he looks like he could handle anything. All of this settles the decision for me. Turning around, I kneel on the bench and make sure to hike up my tight skirt.

Good thing I shaved and let's not forget the fact that I'm wearing my favorite purple lace and satin thong. My ass? I'm actually proud of that part of my body. Due to lots of squats it's tight. Big…but tight.

And if he thinks I'm embarrassed presenting myself to him? Then he's wrong.

I'm not a virgin, but I'm not a whore either. I've had my share of sexual experiences but I also know damn sure that nothing would compare with having sex with this man. Because the way he kissed me? Yeah, talk about exploring all senses, and that's exactly what I'm going to do...explore.

I don't see or hear him and yet I know he's standing right behind me. He's got this vibe radiating off him that reaches something deep inside me. A connection that also scares the crap out of me because it's most definitely captivating enough to reach for my soul and hand it over to this man on a silver platter.

"You better count each time my hand pauses between skin hitting skin or I will start over. Understood?" His voice is solid and yet it tinges with a hint of huskiness that makes goose bumps scatter all over my skin.

I'm still processing his words, the sound of his voice, the electricity that flows around us, when I feel his hand touch my ass. Gently rubbing a circle while his voice turns husky with a hint of laughter. "That would be 'yes, sir' or if you'd like to please me, use 'yes, master' but like I said…this is my last night here. I never allow any sub to call me by my name when I do a scene with them. But you're not a sub, are you?"

Dammit, is that a trick question? Why are we even having this discussion? Why can't he spank my ass already or better yet…screw me silly. Yes. Screw me silly, Calix. Would that answer please him?

Hot.

Fire.

That's the answer my ass is getting from my unspoken question. Ho-ly-shit. How big is his hand? Count. I needed to count, right? "One." I breathe, proud of myself I managed to cut loose some of my working brain cells to save my ass. Well, not so much save my ass because…ouch. "Two."

It's a blur of heat when more smacks rain down while they zing to pleasure. I'm actually regretting saying fifteen when he's done. Yet he isn't done completely. Both his hands are rubbing slow circles over my ass. He didn't smack just one cheek, he switched between both and even hit the curve underneath.

All of this feels like he's in full control and

dammit, I'm moaning and pressing back, just hoping his hand will move lower. If he'd only stroke my clit then I'm sure I'll orgasm with just a mere touch.

His fingers dig into my skin, pinning me in place. "No, Ten. That's not what this was about."

Ten. Did he just call me Ten? No one calls me that. It's either my full name or VP. Oh, and my father calls me by my middle name, Cerise...but no else does, it's always been Tenley, never Ten. And dammit, that's not the reason why I'm annoyed. It's because he won't let me come.

"Maybe we should make an exception," I fire back.

"About what, Ten?" His finger pulls up my thong and he lets it slap back in place. "About your needs? About the fact that your arousal is wafting up, letting me know how much you've enjoyed your punishment? Or the fact that you haven't apologized yet?"

Shit. Is this guy for real? "I'm sorry, Calix. Clearly, I didn't know how much you value people to be civil around you. But seriously, though...you're a biker, how do you handle all your brothers? They can't really all be," Dammit, yet again fire flames through my already flaming ass. "Shit, I told you I was sorry, why did you do that for?"

I look over my shoulder but Calix has his eyes fixed on my ass as if it's the most exquisite and rarest thing he's seen in years. My throat becomes dry enough that I have to cough, causing him to lock eyes with me.

A smirk slides in place. "You have a gorgeous ass. Anyone ever tell you that?"

"No." And why do I sound breathless when he's staring at me like that?

"Then you must have only dated men who don't appreciate a fine woman when it's displayed right in front of them," the man with so many tattoos, muscles, and the rest of his rugged model features states.

"I don't date. The few I've had run-ins with were facing me, and were not very talkative besides the 'so good' and 'that's it baby'." Crap. Did I really just say that? But that does sum up my sexual experiences to the tee.

The muscle in his jaw jumps. "Let me guess, no orgasm thrown in the mix with those run-ins, right?"

He's radiating anger and this is the first time I've seen this emotion hitting his features instead of just a fragment in his eyes. Power. In the world I'm a part of it's like ninety-five percent male but never have I've seen anyone who radiates controlled power within such intensity. With this I only manage to nod because he's right…the first time I was drunk and didn't even remember getting into bed with the guy. The next morning when he rolled me over I was so stunned and still dazed it was all done and over within a few minutes.

Since then I have a distaste for men, especially for Dane Gilton. But like I said…in my life I'm surrounded by bikers so the alpha, badass, dirty mouth routine gets old and the appeal is lacking but this man standing behind me? The one placing his hard, muscled, leather covered thigh between my legs and putting pressure on my clit? I'd gladly surrender to him.

His fingers grip my thigh to keep me in place while he slowly rocks his leg, creating delicious friction. "That's it, Ten. Aw, look how your arousal is making my thigh glisten. That might be the most perfect vision I've seen in months." His hand slides up and down my spine, over the laces of my corset until his fist grips my hair. "You're going to come for me, right, sweetness?"

Oh, shit. That voice. A rumble that's filled with

longing and demand. The friction with added pressure on my clit, his scent…leather, spicy yet clean… it's everything that he wraps me in. My skin feels too tight, heat flaming on the inside with the kind of electricity that shoots from my clit into a thousand pieces highlighting my entire body.

"Calix!" I scream and moan long and loud while he holds on to my body.

There's nothing to compare this with. My whole life was just turned upside down by one freaking orgasm. That's it. I think I'll just stay here for about a week to get my strength back. That's how long my nap will take because the work I just put in…the energy that was drained right out…yeah…long nap, coming right up.

"Sweetness, are you falling asleep on me here?" Damn that man and his sexy chuckle pulling me from my nap because that hot breath right next to my ear? Goose bumps.

That might be the only thing I want besides a nap; more. *More of him.*

"Come on, Ten." Freaking hot fire, my ass.

"Stop smacking my ass, dammit." Ouch. I should

have known he'd smack me again for that.

I glare over my shoulder and watch how he steps away from me. Shit. There's a glistening spot on his thigh. That's me. I did that. My arousal is all over his leather pants. He can't wash that off, right? Yikes. How many times has he done that? Oh, gross…I might have cooties.

"That." I point at his thigh. "Do I need to wash up now? Get disinfected? Ugh, I'm so stupid."

"Stop," Calix snaps and narrows his eyes. His fingers wrap around my neck as he pulls me close enough so he's towering over me, our noses almost touching. "I never get close enough to get a woman's arousal on my leathers. You'd better stop with insulting me or you won't be able to sit for a week, do you understand me?"

"Yes," I hiss through clenched teeth. "How am I supposed to know that, huh? All I see is you, this place, and what just happened? I don't know…it's…" I try to swallow my next word because I can hardly say it's too, "Embarrassing." Dammit. It's his eyes I tell you, they suck the honesty right out of me.

Making me want to blurt out my whole life's

experience so he can take me on his lap and tell me life will be better from now on because he will be there. Holy hell on Earth I need to run away from him and the fairytale bubble he surrounds me with.

"Very good, Ten. Very good. Your honesty pleases me. I think you deserve a reward for that." Husky. That man has more tones to his voice then all the colors of the rainbow.

And I just might adore every freaking one. But right now, I'm like a kid in a candy store and I want my freaking reward. Like I said…if he continues with this I might just admit to anything if he keeps those orgasms flowing.

His eyes slide to my mouth while inching closer. Time seems to stop and the fine line between right or wrong, good or bad, evaporates. I don't care that I just met him. There's only me, him, and our mouths exchanging the most intense pleasure that I never thought could be possible with just a mere kiss.

My hands run over his leather cut, gripping it to get closer to him. His chest rumbles with a sound so primal and loud enough that I can feel the vibrations rippling through my breasts. We're practically merging together and yet I feel like we're not close enough.

He catches my bottom lip between his teeth and pulls it gently before letting go. Soft kisses trail a path to my ear where his hot breath strokes my skin. "I want nothing more than to make you come around my cock, Ten. But you have to earn that."

Thoughts run through my head, from *'what an egocentric ass'*, *'the fuck did he just say?'* and *'is he kidding me?'* to *'I wonder what it would take to earn that privilege'*. Oh, yes…I'm a goner when it comes to Calix. This man is seriously dangerous and now I understand why my father wanted me to bring him in. I'm guessing this man can do, and will get, everything he wants.

His mouth is sucking my neck hard enough for me to know he's leaving a mark. I'm too caught up in the way the sensation ripples straight through my clit to care about it. Tilting my head to the side to give him more room while I moan out my gratitude.

"That's just it, sweetness…something tells me you will earn it soon enough." He freezes up, and mutters, "Fuck."

He takes a step back and coldness instantly wraps around me.

His hand plows through his short, thick hair. I openly ogle how the muscles flex on his inked forearm. "We need to talk first. The both of us are getting carried away here. Come on. Let's get changed before I rip you out of that corset and...yeah, we better leave."

I'm two seconds away from jumping on the bed while I spread my legs and scream 'take me now, dammit' but that would be silly. No. That would be pathetic. Yes, I've lost my mind. He's right, we need to get out of here.

I wiggle my hips while pulling down my tight skirt. The man is relentless, smirking at me like that.

"Save it," I snap. "We're getting out of here so we can have a normal talk without sexual distractions."

"That would be best," he croaks and slides his tongue over his bottom lip. And then he's on me again.

My back hits the door while I'm being caged by his strong body. One hand fisting my hair, guiding my head as he dominates my mouth. The fingers of his other hand are digging in my thigh as he lifts up my leg. I'm fighting his tongue, we're participating in a dance that's driven by the lust that's flaming between us.

My nails dig into his neck, trailing up through his hair. He groans in approval when I sneak a hand over his tight leather covered ass. Man, that's one hell of a hard ass. Powerful. Muscled. I bet he can last hours while thrusting inside me. Oh, how I would like to put that to the test.

He rotates his hips, letting me feel the big, solid length that he's got hidden inside that leather pants of his. That's one huge surprise he's got locked up in there, that's for sure. He wraps his fingers around my neck, keeping me pinned, letting me know he's in full control. This makes me slide my hand in between us to stroke the huge bulge, letting him know some part of him is ready to let things go out of control.

His lips are ripped from mine as he places his forehead on my shoulder. "You're destined to be the one who's going to breach all my damn boundaries, woman. So. Fucking. Tempted. To give in." He releases a deep sigh. "I'm taking you back to my place where we're going to have a long chat, and then we're going to get this over with. Fuck once, or even if it takes a whole night of fucking, we're going to get it out of our system. Understood?"

"Yes. That would solve my itch com-freaking-pletely." I sigh in relief. "Now, distance. Please, or we won't get out of here and you'll be using that mouth for other things." I pat him on the back but stop when his head comes into view.

Oooops. His left eyebrow raises in question, a clear indication he's questioning my sanity because obviously I overstepped. Freaking Dom. What was it my friend told me? Eyes down make him feel like he's running the show.

"Your logic, sir. My own mouth just got a little excited." My head goes down to inspect the nice stilettoes I'm wearing.

Yup, I got some of my sanity back. Mental note to thank my friend later. She gave me a speed course of the things she learned during training. A sub always needs to keep a Dom happy. Not that I have any ambitions to become a sub. Though if it involves getting some serious action from the man in front of me? I obviously wouldn't mind keeping this Dom happy... and myself too while I'm at it.

CHAPTER THREE

CALIX

I bet my hard as steel cock this woman in front of me knows very well what she's doing right now. Saying the perfect things and her body reacting like I would expect from a submissive. On one side my cock is itching to get wet, on the other side, though? I liked her way more without the act. Though it's fun to punish a sub who's trying to manipulate her Dom, I'd rather have her the feisty way.

Dammit, I feel less and less like myself. I used to get pumped up stepping into this club, loving the lifestyle. Yet now it feels like everything in my damn life is lacking. Well, except for this woman in front of me, if she drops the sub act that is, because I can see her glaring at me through her lashes and that right there spikes my heartrate. Yeah, maybe not everything in my life is lacking now that she walked into it.

"Out the door with that sore ass of yours before I give you another ten for trying to manipulate your Dom." I can't help but smirk at the way she narrows her eyes at me. "Oh, yes, sweetness...I know every trick in the book. You'd have to either be very smart, or very well trained, to slip past my guards."

"Noted," she snaps and stalks out the door.

I wait a moment to watch that tight ass all perky from the way her long legs lift that shit up with her stiletto heels, before I fall into step behind her. Regret flows through my veins for not tapping that sweet pussy. And it is a damn sweet pussy because I've got a stain on my leather pants that I'm wearing with pride. I can still smell her damn arousal, like she left me wrapped in it, to tempt me.

I shake my head and follow her in the direction of the locker rooms. Esmee is sitting behind the desk again when we walk past it. Ten walks into the locker room but stalks right back out.

"What's up?" I question.

She looks around me, probably in the direction where Esmee is sitting. "My friend's not there to help me out of the corset. Never mind, I'll ask Esmee."

Nope. That's not happening. "Turn around." I make sure to put enough dominance in my voice so she doesn't even think of defying me.

Like the artic just froze up all over in her magnificent blue eyes. I grab her upper arms and spin her around before I reach down and grab my knife out of its special holster on my boot and flip it open.

"Stay perfectly still," I tell her and the gasp that leaves her throat lets me know she feels the cold steel of my knife as I cut away the laces of the corset. "There. And no worries. I'll buy you a new one."

She spins around, her arms gripping her bosom. "Don't bother. I won't be coming here again."

The first thing that races through my head is 'thank fuck' because for some reason I don't want her here. In my bed? Hell to the fuck yes. In here for all to see? Fuck, no. Again, dual emotions fill me up. Dammit, am I getting old? Ready to head over to Florida to soak in the sun and retire? I need to take a breath and get some distance between us.

"Go change. I'll do the same and we'll meet right here," I tell her and stalk off to get my clothes out of my own locker in the men's changing room.

Changing fast, I grab my bag with the change of clothes I just stashed in there and glance inside my locker where my bag sits with all my damn toys and equipment. I debate what to do and without realizing it, I've locked my locker and walk out without it. I don't even have time to lean against the wall to wait for Ten because she strolls right out in front of me.

Ten is wearing leather pants that were made for that tight ass of her. She's got a leather jacket on, like me, and she's wearing her cut over it, again…like me. She turns and my heart gets jabbed with an electric current. The VP patch on her tit is there, clear as day…a damn fine woman, and a motherfucking VP of an Areion Fury chapter. How the hell is that even possible?

For these last few months I've felt life and meaning slip from my fingers. The vision in front of me is like an inferno of challenges that rips away all boundaries. Boundaries I itch to find new ways to put back in place. She's like a damn unsolvable puzzle that will keep my mind occupied for a lifetime. I need this challenge and I'm already set to face anything she's going up against.

We stroll out and I check the parking lot while I ask, "How did you get here?"

She points to the side where I've parked my bike and I now see one that's parked next to mine.

"That one's mine," she states.

That's an oldie. "Is that a BMW R80 RT? What year?"

"1982," she says with a tiny smile.

"Nice choice," I say and stalk over to mine, stashing my bag into one of the saddlebags.

"Custom Harley for you, huh?" She eyes the bike I've rarely been riding.

I usually take my Aston Martin but I totaled it a few weeks ago and haven't thought of buying a new car. I just started riding my bike again.

"That's right." I give her a wink and add, "Try to keep up, sweetness." I hit the throttle and gain speed, heading for my Prez's house.

My heart is pounding in my chest with just the thought that she's behind me on her bike. I don't look back and she doesn't pass me until we hit a red light. She comes up next to me and places her boot on the ground. I lick my damn lips at the sight of her on that bike. She doesn't spare me a glance, her eyes set on the traffic lights. That's the whole reason I fail to take lead when she speeds off.

All worth it because now I get to be on her ass. She's one damn fine vision when she leans into the curb, going around the corner so smooth, my dick hardens even more. Yes. I have a boner with just watching her ride and let me tell you something…it's damn uncomfortable. I'm happy when my Prez's house comes into view. Ten is already swinging her leg off her bike when I park next to her.

"How did you know where I was heading?" I question.

The corner of her mouth twitches. "My dad told me where you lived. You headed into the other direction and I happen to know where Zack and Blue live." She shrugs. "Easy enough."

"That it is," I tell her and shoot a message to Zack, letting him know I'm here.

I'd ring the doorbell but my Prez is a bit on edge

with his ol'lady on the verge of popping out twins. I don't want to interrupt her sleep or anything, it's late enough as it is. The door swings open and it's not Zack but a very pregnant Blue standing there trying to rip my eardrums out with her high pitch squeal before she tries to hug Ten. That belly of hers getting in the way of dragging her close.

"Get into the house, dammit," Zack growls from behind Blue. "You're not wearing socks."

Is this man for real? There's protectiveness and there's exaggeration. This man is balancing on insanity when it comes to his woman.

"Oh, hush, I'm not complaining about cold feet, am I?" Blue mutters while she pulls Ten into the living room.

Zack closes the door behind me and whispers, "You just wait, it will be less than five damn minutes before she asks me to turn on the heat because she's cold. The damn woman is always cold."

I shake my head while wearing a smile. "I need to have a word with you, is it okay we go into your office?" I ask him.

"Sure, one sec," Zack states and just stands there…

waiting…on…what?

"Zack, sweetie, can you turn on the heat? It's a bit chilly in here," Blue asks in a sweet tone.

Zack on the other hand has his eyes wide, hands palms up and out in front of him in a 'for Christ's sake I told you so' movement.

I'm having a hard time keeping my laughter to myself. I don't have to mention to Ten that I need a private discussion with Zack. For one, that's none of her business, but it's mainly because she's wrapped up in a deep discussion with Blue.

Blue's got the tips of her hair dyed blue, leaving the rest a bright blonde. Ten's hair seems blonde but when the wind blows, the lilac underneath shines through. Or when I fist it, the bright color will seep through my fingers. Shit. I need to put a pin in those thoughts.

Zack leads the way to a room down the hall he uses as his office. Dropping himself in the chair behind his desk he waits for me to take a seat before he gestures with his hand for me to start.

"That's Big Oaks daughter in there, asking for my help." I keep my eye on my Prez who doesn't even seems surprised.

"I know," he simply states.

"You know?" I snap. Somewhat pissed at the fact that I come bringing old news.

Zack pins me with a glare. "Didn't the welcome Blue gave her state the obvious? Those two have met a few times already over the last few months. You know how it is, Calix. Shit rarely passes by a Prez if another chapter wants to reach out to a biker that doesn't belong to them."

Dammit. He's right. "Well, that's all I know about that woman, so feel free to fill me in what you've heard."

He releases a deep sigh and places his forearms on the desk, leaning in to face me head on. "Before I tell you, there are a few things I need to get off my chest first. So, shut up and listen. The last few months I've seen you change. And I'm not talking about you inking yourself beyond what the suit can hide from plain view. I couldn't care less that your hands are inked and your damn neck for that matter...but that's it right? Sealing the deal to back away from it? Turning in your badge, quit bartending at the Purple Bean, signing over your club Ares. You're bored, Calix. You need a challenge.

And I believe a challenge just reached out that would be perfect to get you back on track."

I really hate that man. Sometimes I feel like Zack is a pussy. That Blue would be more capable to run this MC with the type of balls that chick has...but the fact is...Zack is right. I am bored of how my life is going these last few months. Nothing is appealing. Except for the ten types of dynamite that's sitting in the living room right now, waiting for me.

I rub a hand down my face before I say, "Tell me what you know."

"Doctors gave Big Oaks a few months, a year, tops. His kidneys turned to shit among other things, but he basically told me he's old and his time has come. Tenley knows her dad is sick but not to what extent. They both don't want Dane Gilton taking over. He's a bad seed they haven't had a chance to get rid of. You know Dane is Willy's kid. Willy being one of the first who founded the Ohio chapter...Big Oaks couldn't vote him out with his father, the VP, sitting next to him at the table. Then Willy died, and through an opportunity Tenley proved herself and became the VP. Dane wants her as his Ol'lady and wants to rip the gavel out of

Big Oaks' hands. Big Oaks caught Dane messing with his meds. He didn't tell Tenley but reached out to me. Only Feargal and Hugo are aware Dane wants Big Oaks dead so he can take his place. He wants you, Calix. He's always seen you as someone who should be Prez, and to be honest? You fucking deserve to be one. You're capable as fuck and in this moment in life I'm dead sure you need it."

I'm out of my chair with my next breath. "You want me to head out and grab that gavel, snatch up that Prez patch and sow it on my pecs?"

"What?" Tenley gasps.

She's standing in the doorway, clearly hearing me state the shit I was repelled by. That was the damn reason I voiced it back to Zack. I've been close to being a VP once, but a Prez? That's not something that's been on my mind the last years, that's for sure.

"Now just wait a goddamned minute," I growl, trying to contain this situation that I've clearly lost control over when her fist hits my jaw.

Dammit. What's with her and punching dudes in the face? I snatch both her wrists and manage to spin her around while I cage her against my body.

"Calm down, Ten. I was getting intel from Zack and stating stuff back that he told me. I don't have any damn ambitions to snatch the Prez patch from your father. Now sit down and listen in for all I care but be civil or I'll drag you over my damn lap and spank your ass if you attack me again. Clear?"

I shove her away from me and she turns to face me head on, standing on her damn toes to snarl in my face but before she can, I wrap my fingers around her throat and give a slight squeeze. "Remember, sweetness. Be. Civil."

The heat of the flames that are shooting from her eyes? That shit is giving the skin on my face third degree burns. Truth is...I fucking revel in it.

Underneath my fingers I feel her heartbeat pick up. I lean closer and tell her, "I don't want it, Ten. But even more? Ohio's still got a Prez I respect more than my own damn father. The only one close to having that kind of respect is standing behind the desk over there. And now that we've got this cleared up, either sit down and shut up, or go back to the living room because Zack and I aren't done yet."

Her brow wrinkles in confusion. "You're giving

me a choice?"

I poke a finger against her firm bosom where the VP patch is. "This ain't just a piece of fabric, right?"

She steps away from me and plunks down in a chair, crossing one very sexy leg over the other. I'm fighting a damn smile as I face my Prez who does nothing to hide his smirk. His face clearly telling me shit I'm not ready to accept.

"What's your thoughts about handling Dane, Prez? You've known longer than me what he's been up to, any ideas yet?" I ask.

"You need to step up, but I don't want you going in alone, not when a chapter is this unsteady. C.Rash will go with. See how Ransom is doing. He can't ride a bike but it might be good to drag him along so he can plant his ass in the clubhouse to have your back." Zack taps his finger on his desk. "You've gotta be careful, Calix. We don't know how far Dane's reach is. Big Oats said Dane didn't have a lot of bikers backing him up but you never know with this shit." Zack eyes Ten and I damn well know what he means.

By the look on Ten's face she's fully aware too. "Go on, say it...it's because of me. No one likes a woman as a VP. Cunts are only good for one thing, right? Well, when they don't have an ol'lady status that is. But that's where this all started, because I turned down Dane and his ego is crushed. Fucker."

Slowly, I turn my gaze to her and ask, "Mind expanding on that topic?"

Her eyes narrow. "What? That guys like to screw? Either with my pussy, mind, or my damn life? Long story short, Dane thought he could claim me as his ol'lady after one night I landed in his bed and couldn't even remember how I got there in the first place. He vowed he would make my life a living hell if I didn't become his ol'lady. You know...because his father used to be VP, entitled to step up as Prez when the time comes."

I groan internally. It's one huge soap opera and they want to drag me into that shit. Wait. "What was that about a night you couldn't remember?"

"Nothing," Ten snaps. "One drink too many, never made that kind of mistake? Stick with the basics. Dane needs to back off. He's never going to be president. He already took it to the table once, demanded a vote, he didn't even gain more than five votes."

"Who were the five?" Zack asks. "We need to know who has his back."

"Ryke, Steel, Beck, Hank, and Bo," Ten states like it doesn't affect her.

Yet I damn well know it does, because, "Beck? Really? Big Oaks practically raised that sonofabitch."

"Yeah, well, what other option is there? A Prez with a cunt? Dane can smooth talk those brothers into having a higher status in the club than they have now. Or make changes, take risks, that Big Oaks never would do or take." Ten swallows the rest of her words and it may seem like she's ready to raise hell, but I can see right through that shit.

She's breaking. It's personal. I'm very aware and Big Oaks might not have been completely honest to her about his health, but she ain't stupid either. With him gone...what does she have left? Because I know Big Oaks lost his ol'lady to cancer seven years ago. Her mother.

She doesn't have anyone except for the MC. An MC with a biker who wants her as his personal fuck hole while screwing everything else in sight. Because I know how Dane is, he likes his variety in pussy.

He was an asshole back when I knew him and I'm pretty damn sure he only got worse over time by the sound of it.

I stand up and hold out my hand. "I gave you an option. You chose me. So that's it, sweetness. Let's go. I need to grab some stuff from my place before we head over to yours."

Relief washes over her. She stands up and takes my hand, shaking it once before letting it drop. "Let's go, slick. We have some business to settle."

Slick? I'll show her slick. I remember the agreement we had before we got here. Something about scratching an itch to get both our rocks off. Good thing we're headed to my house. Perfect place to settle the score before heading out of town to handle Dane once and for all.

CHAPTER FOUR

TENLEY

I'm still annoyed by the fact that Zack and Calix had a little moment of whispering to one another when Zack handed Calix an envelope right before we left. Clearly, they didn't want me listening in because when I stepped closer, Calix told me to stay put. And let me tell you, when he uses his voice in that sharp and hard tone? Every cell in my body dances to his tune only. It's insane. That man has way too much effect on me.

It's strange. I've been around lots of bikers my whole life and yet this one manages to bring my body alive. I know my dad and him go way back...but that was before I was even allowed to be at the club.

My mom kept me away when I was a teenager and it's only been seven years since I've been helping out around there. First with handling the business, chipping in because they were making a mess with the administration.

My mom used to keep everything in line but when she became very ill she couldn't and everyone just neglected that task. After the funeral I needed something to do. I was done with school and wanted to make myself useful. I even made a business plan to turn things around for the MC. Well, with hard headed bikers no one wanted to give me the time of day when I told them I thought of something to make good cash. In the end? I really showed them…it earned me my VP patch.

"Are you coming up or are you going to stay here until I've packed a bag?" Calix's voice rips me out of my thoughts.

"Yeah, let's see your apartment, slick." And I am kinda curious because this guy is like an enigma.

Hot to cold, all stuck to principle, that's all I've summed him up to till now. Checking out his apartment would surely give more insight to this man.

With all that muscle and ink, his bike, his house…
nothing makes sense. His apartment is in a building
that looks more like a high-class hotel. We went into
an underground garage to park our bikes. This whole
floor is filled with expensive cars.

We step inside the elevator. Calix takes out a key
card and doesn't even press a button to get the elevator
to move. It's a quick trip to what I now become aware
is the top floor. When the doors open, I realize we're
stepping straight into Calix's apartment.

"Penthouse, huh?" I give him a wink and whistle at
the amazing view.

I'm thankful Calix doesn't flip the lights on but
leaves the room dark as I walk right up to the floor to
ceiling windows. Bright city lights that paint an amazing décor of depth. I could stand here for hours just
enjoying this view.

"Magnificent, right?" Calix's voice whispers from
behind me.

I can feel him standing close to me.

"Breathtaking. I think that's one of the most exquisite views I've ever seen," I admit.

His fingers slide my hair away from my neck,

making a free path for his nose that's now trailing my neckline.

"You don't know half the things I would do to you," Calix murmurs, immediately putting my body on edge.

"Tell me," I breathe.

"You smell so good. Makes me want to trail my tongue over every single inch of your body. To kiss, lick, suck, but most of all…I want to bite you. And I don't mean a little nip either. I want to really sink my teeth into your delicate skin so you will carry my mark for days. Just the thought gets my cock even harder, because, Ten. Feel." He grabs me by the hips and grinds himself against me.

Making me fully aware how huge, and mostly, how hard his erection is. I shiver from the promise in his words. Even if he's doing nothing more than roaming his hands over my body, his lips feathering over my skin…I can feel myself getting wet. I shouldn't do this. I should keep my brain functioning. I hardly know him…my father trusts him, vouches for him… what the hell am I doing?

"I can feel you," he whispers. "I can taste your heartbeat with my tongue, feel your thoughts invading your body. I should tell you to stop thinking, but I like the mouth you have and your feistiness." He nips my damn ear after the whisper of words on a hot breath.

A moan escapes me. His chest rumbles with a growl that vibrates through my back. My leather jacket and cut are pulled down, baring my left shoulder before he sinks his teeth into my skin. I gasp due to the flare of pain that flashes to heat, and when his tongue laps lazily over his mark…I all but lean back against him, ready to turn into a puddle of goo in his hands to do with me whatever he feels like.

This man has created a remote and has the ability to push all the right buttons to control my body. I need to snatch back some control; no one owns me. That right there makes me stop in my tracks, spin around and dig my fingers into his cut to drag him closer. Time to turn the tables.

His eyes flare as he just stands there, rising his eyebrow at me before he says, "Well now, that's different." I can tell he's fighting a grin.

"What? Don't tell me no woman has ever," I don't get to finish what I was going to say because he interrupts me.

"Never. Whatever you were going to say I can answer with; none. Not one woman has ever dared to advance, taken the first step, jump me, or even so much as initiated a kiss. I won't allow it, everything always went down the way I allowed it to." He inches forward into my face. "I kinda like your hands on me, taking lead, sweetness." Husky. My skin prickles from the way his words penetrate me. It's like a confession, a plead, a challenge…all of those wrapped in one.

Standing on my toes, I tighten my fists and bring our mouths together. Soft at first but this man unleashes longings deep inside me that boil on the inside, searching for the steam to flow out to release pressure. It's for that reason I nip his bottom lip and give it a tug. I lick away the sting before diving inside in an overwhelming need to taste him.

Sliding one hand up to cup his neck while the other one runs through his short hair that's got just enough length for me to grip. I guide his head to the left so I can deepen the kiss. I did mention he drives me crazy, right? I feel like I need to climb him like a mountain I need to conquer.

He growls into my mouth, grabbing my ass in one swoop that has me automatically wrapping my legs around his waist. The kiss turns from devouring into pure domination where I barely manage to keep up. This man utterly consumes me and yet again I come to a point where within this moment...I don't care, as long as he doesn't stop.

Shit. The doorbell rings and my disappointment is apparently shared with Calix as he growls his frustration into my mouth. He rubs my pelvis against his thick erection before he lets me slide down his body.

"That damn man is never fucking early except now? What the actual goddamned, fucking, hell?" he grumbles and it's now that I realize it's the first time I catch him cursing that much. Even more...he openly shows and voices emotion...so the polite, controlled biker does have the ability to lose control...*nice*.

My heart leaps over the fact that I'm the one who pushed him. He's a man who always seems in total control. The both of us were just as caught up in this moment. That's never happened to me, and I can imagine by Calix's reaction that it's something he's not used to either; we were ready to put our lives on hold so we could create a space that contains just the two of us.

But it also scares me. The only thing I've ever experienced was a crush on a guy I thought was wild and free, someone who would give me everything I gave him in return. In the end he was disgusting, less than nothing, and the biggest asshole that walks this earth. He was a huge mistake, one that still haunts me.

I need to be careful with Calix. And, dammit, my dad and his bright ideas. Now I wonder if he set me up...no, he wouldn't...would he? Yikes. No way would my dad go boyfriend hunting for me. Or in our terms... hook me up with an ol'man. Dammit, when I think about it even more…yeah…he would.

No...Calix doesn't strike me as a man who would let someone hook him up. He glances up to a screen on the wall that shows a biker standing in the elevator. Calix strolls over and allows the elevator doors to open so the guy can step inside the apartment.

Calix flips on the lights, making the guy chuckle. "Sorry, man. Seems like I've interrupted your playtime, huh? I'm early, I know. But when Zack told me I was heading to the Ohio chapter, I jumped into action.

It's been years since we've been there. Can't wait."

"Rein it in, C.Rash. You were a baby back then, a prospect who couldn't keep his cock in his pants. That's not what I need. I need someone that has my back because shit is about to flare up there. I need my eyes up ahead, I don't have time to keep watch over you, boy." Calix's voice has turned cold at the end, a loud and clear warning.

Every inch of desire and emotion inside my body toward this man flushes away with the reality of why I came in search of Calix in the first place. I need backup. I need more than one reliable person, some-one who's capable of handling anything. Because I know for sure Dane would gladly kill my father who he thinks is warming the president chair for him.

Another reality is that my father is dying. He might think he's keeping it from me, how bad his heath has gotten, but that's not something one can hide. Not when I'm living with him and can see it with my own eyes. Well, and the fact I found the letters from the hospital and the bills along with it.

"I'm aware, I'm just excited. You know that, I've got your back at all times, brother," the guy Calix called C.Rash says. "Dams is coming with too. He'll be joining us for about two weeks I think, and Tyler will drive back and forth to relieve him if we need to stay longer."

"I'm aware. I've requested the VP tag along, his opinion is vital for me." Calix keeps his eye on me when he says this and it makes me wonder what it entails.

My skin prickles with awareness that I can't place. I feel as if the last few hours were a whirlwind that spun my life into another dimension. Nothing makes sense since this guy came into my life. I need to get back home, at least there I've got my dad to turn to for advice and strength. I would say it's where I feel safe, but I guess Dane fucked that up a long time ago and recently, when I became the VP, it got worse.

Calix steps toward me, grabs my upper arm and guides me down the hall. "Stay put C.Rash, we'll be right back."

C.Rash says something along the lines of not having a problem with us having a quickie while he waits on the couch.

"What the hell do you think you're doing?" I ask

him while I yank my arm from his grip and spin around.

"Grabbing my stuff so we can get out of here, but I need to ask you some questions so I'm multitasking." He stalks over to a closet and pulls out a large bag and starts to fill it with jeans and some Henleys.

"What questions? And aren't you going to throw in some underwear?" Why did I pop out that question? But for real...the man went from jeans, to Henleys, to throwing in a large box of condoms. Uh huh, I didn't question the condoms...I guess I'm the weird one here, right?

"I turned in my badge, became a silent partner in my own damn club I've owned for years, and quit my bartending job. I'm not wearing my suits anymore where I needed underwear. I've never worn boxers underneath jeans, so no...no underwear. Unless," He pins me with a stare. "Do I need to bunk with your dad, or sleep on his couch? Then I might need some boxers. He always did freak out if brothers were walking around naked."

His statement makes me snort and shake my head. "True. That hasn't changed. And probably the reason why he didn't allow me in the clubhouse until seven years ago. If you're planning on staying with us, then you need boxers. We do have a spare bedroom though."

"We?" Calix's eyebrow shoots up. "You live with your dad fulltime, no apartment on the side?"

"Nope. I never moved out. All I've been doing all my life is study and after that work. I took care of my mom and dad every step of the way as they've done so for me." I feel a proud smile sliding on my face.

Because for sure I am proud. Of what my parents taught me, life lessons, and their guidance. I owe them so much and giving something in return, anything, no matter how small or how big, is a privilege.

Calix steps up and brushes his knuckles against my cheek. "Absolutely stunning when you light up like that. Adoration, pride, longing, love, so many powerful emotions right on display. It's rare you know...throwing that door open to allow a person to get a glimpse of your soul."

I swallow hard and step away while I mutter, "Don't forget to pack underwear and a toothbrush," before I practically run out of the bedroom but I turn in the doorway, suddenly realizing he mentioned turning in his badge. "Wait…you were a cop?"

He gives me a slight smile with a wink before he says, "A detective."

Biting my lip, I let my eyes slide over his appearance. Fully inked, from his hands up to his throat, two days' worth of scruff decorating his hard jaw, short dark hair. No. I clearly can't picture him as a detective, yet he does hold the kind of authority that states he can do anything.

"How many different kinds of handcuffs does a guy need in a lifetime?" Ugh, again with my insane brain wrapping around the fact that this guy owns a BDSM club where they use them and did the line of work where they used them for other purposes.

And why does my body decide to be utterly turned on by that little fact? I mean it's not like I crave to be shackled and incapable of…yeah, scratch that, because that would be thrilling to be at the mercy of this inked up muscled mass of a man who always seems in perfect control.

"If I would slide my hand down your panties, I would find you wet with anticipation. Right, Ten?

Because I can assure you I still have handcuffs. Though I won't use them on you. I would grab both wrists in one hand, hold them pinned above your head as I keep your body hostage with mine. You see, I've got many ways to make you light up, sweetness. To prepare your body in a way where you're begging me to stop, pleading to surrender to the kind of pleasure no man has ever given you."

He's standing on the other side of the room and yet it feels like he's got his hands all over my body, lighting it up with the promise of just mere words. This man is dangerous in many ways but mostly…he's a hunter that would eventually capture my heart, conquer it for safe keeping, slaying every threat in its perimeter.

Shit. That's exactly why I need to focus. Every damn time this man seems to make me forget everything other than the need to spread my legs. "Let's cut this short. Clearly, we need to fuck and get this itch scratched we both seem to have when we're near each other, but I have other things to deal with that are more important. You're distracting and making me feel out of balance. So, this," I wave a hand back and forth between him and me, "we're going to put a pin in it and when everything is handled, we'll go for a few rounds of sex so the both of us can be on our merry way again."

I blink twice before he's in front of me, pulling my body out of the doorway, pressing me against the wall as he shuts the door with a loud bang. Fury invades his eyes and his chest is heaving rapidly. His body is flaring up, all the signs that I've struck a nerve and he's barely keeping a handle on his always calm demeanor.

"Why the fuck do you always have to push my damn buttons, Ten? Even if I've got a guy trying to kill me in front of me, a knife in hand ready to strike when I've got no weapons other than my bare hands to fight back…not even then, do I feel any-fucking-thing. Yet you? You seem to pull all my nerve wires and yank the fucking shit out of them. Do you really think I want a quick fuck to get it out of my system? Guess again, sweetness, because before you waved that pretty tight ass in front of me, my life has been a boring gray mass. You spike colors that I never knew existed. And you dare say *I'm making you feel out of balance*? Try imagining how I fucking feel. So yes, we need to handle a lot of things before we will deal with us, but I can assure you that there's no damn way I will put a pin in it. Unless it's my cock that will be doing the pinning, then I'm all for it."

He doesn't even allow me to speak but crashes his mouth over mine. His tongue enters my mouth and dances viciously around with the kind of intensity that has me digging my nails into his skin. This man drives me completely insane.

Calix pulls back just as abruptly but grips my neck, lifting my chin with his thumb to make our eyes lock. "Don't fight me on this because you won't like the punishment I have in mind." A smirk paints his sexy lips. "Ah, you like that thought, don't you? Eyes dilating beautifully, your heartbeat picking up speed underneath my fingers. You're so damn responsive. You're right. We need to focus on the tasks at hand but after that…all bets are off. You'll be mine, clear?"

CHAPTER FIVE

CALIX

I voiced the words over my goddamn lips I never thought would slide right out; you'll be mine. She might as well take it as a spoken claim. To her. Ten. Though she might shove those words away and give them a different meaning. One where she's mine to finally fuck. Make no mistake…that's gonna happen too, but that would only be the start of it.

She's the complete package. It's like a crystal in the sun. Every time you shift it slightly, the sparks will radiate in a whole different way where you discover yet again the beauty of it all. That's her. Surprising, refreshing, feisty, hot, and from what I've heard…

she's also got a damn fine brain. All the reasons to grab what's right in front of me.

But I also saw the shock in her eyes. Before she could get one word over her puffed up, prominent, cherry painted lips, I gave her a quick and hard kiss and told her to wait with C.Rash in the living room so I could finish packing. I had to fight a laugh from slipping out because she was sputtering and waving her hands in protest as I guided her out of my bedroom.

When I walked back into the living room she only gave me hard glares and not one single word. That's fine by me. And the situation stayed like that for hours. Due to the fact that we've been riding since then. Not much discussion time when you're riding a bike. But we just parked our bikes and are heading into the clubhouse of the Areion Fury MC, Ohio chapter.

All kind of feelings hits my chest; recognition, family, brotherhood. This used to be my home. Even now, years and years later, it feels right coming back here. Dams and C.Rash step in behind me as I follow Ten who's heading straight to the left corner where two couches sit across from each other, a few chairs on the left and right with a table in the center. Big Oaks is sitting on one couch, a few bikers are occupying some of the chairs. Among them are Dane, Feargal, Beck, and Hugo.

Hugo's an old friend who was also a prospect around the same time Big Oaks brought me into the club. He jolts up and shouts, "You sonofabitch, about time you dragged your ugly ass back in here."

"Shut it, you ugly mutt. It's been barely three weeks since I last saw you." I act annoyed but on the inside I'm damn excited to see my old friend.

"Three weeks? Try three years, since I ran into you across state lines, fucker. You never call, don't write, no smoke signals, nothing. I thought you died on me." Hugo punches me in the shoulder before he gives me a man hug.

I smack him on the back a few times, grab his shoulders and pull him back, giving him a tiny head-butt. "Damn, I missed your annoying ass, man," I mutter.

"You seriously back for good now? Tell me Big Oaks wasn't fucking lying when he told me you might honor his request," Hugo whispers the words meant for my ears only.

"All in good time, brother," I tell him and watch how Ten plunks down on the couch, sitting across from her father.

I stroll over and sit down right next to her. Dane glares at me. I lean back and spread my arms, draping one over the back of the couch and the other over Ten's shoulder. She spins her head toward me, shooting me a look that states I'm way out of bounds. *I don't fucking care.* I've told her she's mine so I'm openly stating claim. But this might also be a very easy way to ruffle Dane's feathers. Judging from the way Dane's eyes almost pop out of his skull, he got my message loud and clear.

Dane's eyes shift to Ten. "Get up," he hisses through his teeth. "Get up and sit somewhere else."

My fingers tighten around Ten's shoulder. Hoping she's got the logic train of thought that with this action; me laying claim on her. We could draw him out...he'll fuck up much easier when he's mad as hell.

I'm about to calmly address the fucker when Ten surprises the hell out of me. Her hand goes to my thigh as she snuggles against me, ignoring Dane completely. Her eyes find mine as she asks, "Did you want me to grab you a beer?"

The corner of my mouth twitches. Fuck. Even when I know she's playing around, a little show and tell that we've hooked up together…my cock can't tell the damn difference, gorging itself with blood, becoming slightly painful in the confinements of my jeans. Besides…she might be playing, but I'm not.

My fingers find her blonde hair, wrapping it around my fist as I tug her head back and slam my mouth down on hers. My other hand was already reaching for her wrist in case she would push me off, but instead she surprises me yet again when she moans into my mouth and cups my face. Pulling back, she nips my bottom lip.

She stares at my mouth, all play long gone, as she says breathily, "Or you can drink me, whatever."

Laughter rips from my throat. "I'd rather have you any day, all day, sweetness," I tell her honestly, because for real…I can't wait to have her.

A throat clears and then Big Oaks' voice flows through the air. "Okay, you kids, that's enough. There's only so much my stomach can take these days."

I make sure to brush my lips against hers before

I direct my attention on Big Oaks. "Sorry there, Prez. Didn't mean any disrespect."

"None taken, Calix. You might actually make me happy…or not, depending on your answer. What's it gonna be, boy? Scrap metal? Gold? Any idea?" Big Oaks asks.

Brothers are staring at Big Oaks, confused as fuck. I'm not. This is something we used to discuss when I was barely wet behind my ears. A young dude without any experience in life…especially about women. Big Oaks explained it in the way he thought was the best way to get through to me.

Scrap metal being the kind of woman you would go to when you need it, those who you could find anywhere. Silver? The dating kind. Gold? Slap a ring on there. You get the idea. And if you're wondering why the strange comparison…Big Oaks runs a garage and likes all kinds of metal, and sees the use in it.

I take a deep breath and with a huge grin, I let him know. "Platinum."

Although I'd like to say Rhodium, because that's extremely rare and the most valuable kind of metal, but I don't want to confuse the brothers even more than they already are. Again…she might be playing the 'jealousy card' to fuck with Dane's head, that was my intention too, but the end game for me is very different. She'll realize that soon enough though. Hence the reason I refuse to lie to Big Oaks, with Ten being his daughter, he, as well as she, deserves my respect.

A low whistle flows through the clubhouse. "Damn, brother. You ain't fucking around?" Hugo directs at me and lets his gaze land on Dane.

Fuck. I totally forgot Hugo was around most of the time and should know what the hell we're talking about. Doesn't matter, they all will know soon enough. I'm about to say something when Dams reaches forward, breaking the conversation.

"Big Oaks, here's the package you requested. I'm here to oversee the transfer for two weeks and then one of my brothers will come up here if you still need some support. We're looking forward to work with you on this," Dams states.

Ten being the VP, I have no doubt that she knows what this is about, as do I. Both chapters took it to the table a few weeks ago and saw the profit. Though I had no clue about Ten's existence or function within this chapter when we took it to the table. Big Oaks has always kept his personal life separate from the club. Well, not anymore so it seems.

Zack wants to expand the towing business the club owns with Dams' ol'lady, Nerd. Big Oaks owns a garage so it's logical as fuck but Big Oaks hasn't expand in that area yet. This chapter is filled with morons, with a few exceptions, who would rather put their energy into fucking instead of work. Hence the reason money has been tight.

Zack talked to Big Oaks about the idea and he put a file together with all kinds of information. Our MC is going to front the money to invest in a state of the art tow truck, that's going to arrive tomorrow. Dams is here to teach brothers to handle things and I'm sure Pokey, or one of my other brothers will be here in two weeks to take over Dams' job until we're sure they won't fuck up the new truck.

"We don't need no damn babysitters," Dane barks. "We voted it in, we can handle everything ourselves."

I feel Ten go rigid beside me. They took a vote about all of this weeks ago. They voted it in because they all want the cash flow. They've managed to crawl out of debt a month ago but things are still tight, I've seen the books. They launched a new company, a car wash, three months ago and since then they've managed to create a steady income. But they need more. They need this.

"If you would use your brain for two seconds you would understand that setting up a new business entails learning. And when help is offered, you take it and fucking learn. Got it? Be respectful toward your Prez and your brothers, even if they're from another chapter," I tell him in a harsh voice that rings with warning.

If I didn't already hate the fucker, I would have hated him the second I knew he wanted my woman.

I can tell he wants to blow some more steam but the brother I know as Ryke shoves Dane in the shoulder. "Come on, man. Let's get some beers, my throat is dry as an elephant that's crossed the desert."

Dane swings his gaze to Ryke. "That shriveled up hose of yours is always dry. Oh, no wait…that's your cock." Dane snorts and eyes Ten. "We all know mine's been getting wet on a regular basis. Right, Tenley?"

I'm on my damn feet with my next breath.

"Outside, right now. You disrespected your Prez first and now your own damn VP. They may have endured your rude, asshole ways, but that ends this instant," I growl and repeat between clenched teeth, "Outside, Dane. Move."

"I don't answer to you, fucker," Dane snarls.

"You sure about going outside, Calix?" Big Oaks asks me.

I don't take my eyes off Dane, but instead give Big Oaks a tight nod. I don't mean any disrespect, but I won't turn a damn blind eye toward someone I not only despise, but this fucker is one who will kick a man who's down, stick a knife in your back, that kind of sleazy-ass motherfucker. And if the same rules apply as they were years ago when I belonged to this chapter…it's free to challenge another brother to settle a dispute outside.

"Let's go everyone. Dane, Calix, in the ring you two. Bare knuckles, nothing else. Three rounds if you two last that long," Big Oaks states.

Everyone starts to peel out and head outside. This club has a large boxing ring setup behind the clubhouse. One where guys like to go a few rounds of bare hand fighting in when they need to hash something out. Or just for Saturday night's entertainment, whatever. Dane must think I've been out of practice or that he's been training for this because the idiot is gleaming and practically skipping his way to the ring. I'm following the crowd that's heading toward it too when my arm is being pulled.

Glancing down, I see it's Ten who's stopping me. "Why are you doing this?" she whispers, looking around to check and make sure no one heard her.

I reach out and grab her by the back of her neck to pull her close. "He's being disrespectful and needs to be taught a lesson, sweetness. And I can hardly spank him like I did with you because I wouldn't touch that fucker with a ten-foot pole. Unless I'm kicking his ass, so that's exactly what I'm going to do."

"I'm going to be very disappointed if you get your face busted in. Since…you know, I was counting on some more of those kisses. Even if I'm very aware you put on a show to set off Dane." She swallows, her eyes going to the floor as if she's caught herself admitting something she didn't want me to find out.

Placing my thumb underneath her chin, lifting it

slightly up to connect our gaze before I tell her, "I'll make sure we can kiss the fuck out of each other for many lifetimes to come. Back there wasn't just a show. Even if it was, a blind man can see how compatible we are and that's something the both of us can't ignore, we might as well go with it and see how the rest of things fall in place. So, for now, I'm all in and with you demanding some more kisses, I take it you're all in too. Understood?"

Her damn pupils dilate and her gaze slides to my mouth as she whispers, "Understood."

I'm a total fucking goner for this woman right here. I groan and crash my mouth over hers. Reaching for her ass, I grind my rock-hard cock against her. I shouldn't because there's a huge dilemma to deal with when you're about to go into a fight. Can't take a hit to the groin with a damn boner.

But right in this moment? I don't fucking care. Hoisting her up, she wraps her legs around my waist as I carry her toward the boxing ring, resulting in hollers and catcalls from all the brothers around us.

She chuckles into my mouth, pulling back slightly she mutters, "No going back now, huh?"

I know damn well this woman isn't talking about the fight that's about to happen. "Admitting you're my ol'lady already, huh? I must be doing something right." I brush our noses together to tease her some more.

"You're so fucking bad," she says in fake frustration.

"Aw, sweetheart," I groan. "Why do you say that? You haven't even seen me fight or felt me fuck that sweet place between your legs. There will be nothing bad when I open up that slick pussy of yours with my cock so I can feel your tightness wrapped around me. And you will be so fucking tight, I just fucking know it. You, gorgeous, will be deliciously sore after I'm done burying myself over and over until we're both damn sated. The only thing that might be bad is the fact that you're going to be walking funny for a real fucking long time, sweetness."

Ten gasps, "Calix!" And looks around her as if she caught me misbehaving in the middle of a crowd of nuns. "You're really starting to swear and talk dirty out loud."

My head tips back and laughter escapes me. Full blown. I revel in this moment because it's been a long fucking time since I've felt so alive and I owe it all to the woman I'm holding in my arms. The one who I've just called my ol'lady.

"Come on you two," Feargal says. "You need to throat punch that fucker, Calix. Do something a lot of us want to do but haven't had a legit chance…or fuck, not many of us can, so please…shut him the fuck up."

"You got it, Feargal. Do me a favor and keep your eyes on my ol'lady when I'm in that ring," I tell him and see a smile spread over Ten's face.

"Fuck, yeah. I sure will, man. But do me another favor and shout that ol'lady claim out loud so that can be the first punch in the gut that fucker receives. You know how long he's demanded that Tenley was his to claim? He basically stated that ever since he could pull his cock out of his pants. I think that's the best damn below the belt punch you will get in tonight." Feargal chuckles and actually rubs his hands together in excitement.

Feargal's words hit me deep but not because of Dane. It's because of the woman I'm holding. She's been in this life and fought her way into becoming a damn VP in an all man, biker's world. Yet here she is, in my hands, allowing me to kiss the fuck out of her in front of everyone and even managed to claim her as mine. Within a matter of damn hours. Damn lucky she came to search me out at my club. Zack was right…I needed a fucking challenge. Though it's got nothing to do with Dane, but everything to do with my ol'lady; Tenley.

I let her slide down my body, cupping her face in my hands to keep her close. "Stay with Feargal, Dams, and C.Rash. When I step inside that ring I need my focus in there, okay? I know you can handle yourself but I've never had someone who took over my thoughts the way you do. But I need for that to fall away when I'm fighting. One second of lost concentration could mean a blow to the head I won't see coming."

A damn fine smile spreads her face. "Ah, you know just the right choice of words that get me all soft for your rough, hard self, huh? But, yeah…message received, sir."

I groan. "Sweetness, don't address me as sir, and say shit like you getting all soft and me rough and hard, right before I have to step inside a ring to kick someone's ass."

She brushes her lips against mine. "That's a little payback for barging into my life and turning it upside-down."

I smack her ass. *Hard*. Making her stumble even tighter against me. "That's one of twenty you earned for lying. You're the one who came looking for me, remember?"

She's the balance I need. Not a full BDSM relationship but the sweet edge balance of raw fucking, smack that tight ass and tie her up. All of it to prolong the pleasure for the both of us. I don't need the club for that, *all I need is her.*

"My ass will be ready for you…but we might need to schedule it till later because your knuckles might be too bruised. Shit. Let's save this discussion." Her face goes from a sexy flirt to serious as fuck. "Can you do me a favor? Give Dane one hell of a black eye for me. I hate his guts more than you'll ever know."

"It will be my pleasure, sweetness. But remember what I said, stay right next to my brothers, *those I trust,* okay?" I demand with a little snap in my voice to make sure she hears the warning in my words. *I need her safe.*

"Go kick ass, slick. I'll be waiting." She slams her mouth over mine in a hard kiss that catches me by surprise.

But it's over way too soon for me to wrap my hand into her hair the way I like. She's dashing away toward Dams who gives me a nod to tell me he's got her. Time to get my head into the fight. My hands are itching to get some action in. I've been hitting the gym daily and I've never stop training as a fighter, always changing sparring partners.

As a biker, a detective, a bartender, hell even as a fucked-up man who needs to blow off steam; I've needed it. But this right here, inside this ring, there are no limits. It's a 'go all out' kinda thing, and that has been a while for me. I always need to hold back because you can't punch a sparring partner's lights out. It's rude. With this being said…my body is vibrating with the knowledge I can openly punch this fucker's lights out.

I follow the path Ten made because I want her to hold on to my cut. I shrug out of it and hand it over. The wicked woman is actually gleaming with interest as I grab my Henley and pull it over my head.

She snatches it from my hands and slings it over my cut that she's slung over her arm. The lilac fingernails of her right hand trail over my inked chest.

There's a slight tug of uncertainty my heart gives, knowing I have to turn my back on her now and she will see the scars that are all over the skin of my back. No ink can ever hide that shit. I'm not sure how she's going to respond to that. Revolted maybe? But that's a minor concern now. I need to leave that thought because the fight is about to begin, and I can't fucking wait to draw blood. *This fucker is mine.*

CHAPTER SIX

TENLEY

Holy shit. Talk about perfection getting a dent blown into its ego. That's what flashes through my mind when I get a glimpse of Calix's back. Yet those scars are a part of him and seem to balance out the flawless factor. It actually makes me want to get to know him more; what's hidden in this man's soul when he has scars like that.

There isn't a thought in my mind that these scars are inflicted by something from his BDSM club. This because my friend told me all about that lifestyle, that would be a total contradiction to that. For those who scene it's all about the pleasure for both, meaning there's no way those scars are a result of play.

The sight of the scars makes my heart squeeze… I'd like to hear the story behind them. Though I know I can hardly walk up to him and ask about it. Things this crucial make an impact on someone's life. I just have to wait until the right moment comes up, or if he decides to share on his own. All of this makes me aware that I'm more than interested to see how this thing between us will play out in the long run because fire tends to die down once it starts to burn out of fuel…will the sparks that fly between us do the same?

My mind fades back to what's going on in front of me when Calix steps into the ring. Dane is already bouncing on his feet, bare chested and throwing punches in thin air. All I feel for him is repulsion. That wasn't always the case. Hell, no. At one moment in time I had a crush on Dane.

He was one of the bad boy bikers with attitude who made all the girls notice him so yeah…I did too. But that all changed when I had too much to drink, or hell… I only had two or three drinks, I'm obviously a lightweight. I don't even remember how it happened but I ended up in his bed.

I shove down the memory of what happened when I woke up because Hugo steps into the ring and starts to bellow out the rules. Well, basically that there aren't any rules except for maybe poke straight into the eyes and that they need to stop when a man is down. Other than that? The horn indicating it's the end of a round so each of them will go to their corner to take a breath between rounds. The rest is just go full force and don't stop till the three rounds are done.

The horn sounds and Dane bounces around trying to intimidate Calix, who is standing there with his feet slightly spread, his whole posture in utter relaxation except for his hands, they are clenched into fists and ready to strike at any second.

"Why isn't he doing anything?" I mutter in concern.

Dams chuckles beside me. "Patience, Tenley. Look at your ol'man. He's calculating. Taking in every move Dane is making and waiting for his chance to strike at the right time, while Dane on the other hand is all over the place. Challenging, bouncing around to try and throw Calix off his game. He wants to distract him to strike."

This somehow soothes the stress that's building. Ugh, really, Tenley? Jeeeeez, who knew I could actually worry about someone besides my dad and myself after walking into my life like four heartbeats ago? Besides…he's the one who challenged Dane, not the other way around so that means he damn well knows he can take the guy, right?

A gunshot echoes. Everyone goes quiet for a breath or two before shouting and turmoil erupts and I get pushed down while Dams is hovering over me. My eyes never stray from Calix. His relaxed state changing, spinning around to connect his gaze with me.

My heart jolts at the overwhelming tenderness of this gesture, that the first thing on his mind is me... *needing to know that I'm safe.* Yet Dane takes this moment to strike a blow, hitting him hard in the kidney, raining them down one after another. Calix stumbles back, caught by surprise as he braces himself to take the impact of the blows.

"Nooooooo," I scream before I turn my fury at Dane. "You dirty motherfucker! Fucking snake. You're gonna die! Even if I have to kill you with a damn spoon, I'll fucking do it."

Some of the brothers have their guns drawn, ready to handle the threat who caused the gunshot. But I know with Dane's action...jumping Calix like that... that this was a setup. Dane was expecting the gunshot since he was the only one who isn't focused on an outer threat.

I push Dams off me and say, "It was a fucking decoy shot to bring Calix down."

Dams' face is showing the kind of repulsion that's also flowing freely inside me. "That won't go unnoticed, I can fucking guarantee you that." His eyes are focused on something behind me, his mouth turning into a grin. "Although it doesn't matter anyway, look."

Spinning around I need to do a double take. My eyes bounce through the ring to take stock of what happened in the mere seconds I took my gaze off of Calix. Blood is sprayed across the floor of the ring. A few feet from Dane lays the knife that's clearly been used on Calix as a gash on his right arm is freely dripping blood.

But Dane, though? He's on the floor, groaning like he's all spaced out. Calix is standing over him as if he's in a trance. Like a puppet that's waiting for someone to pull the ropes that's tied to his limbs. Because he knows the match is momentarily frozen since Dane is on the floor…he's waiting for Dane to get up so he can pounce some more.

Okay, the puppet thing was a weird comparison due to the fact that there's no one on this damn planet who would be powerful enough to have any hold on this man. He's the epitome of power. Confined strength that's ultimately dosed in the most elegant of ways. Even within this moment he's in full control while I'm standing on the sidelines, fuming on the inside, ready to rip everything and everyone apart who had anything to do with shooting a gun to rig this fight.

A horn blows indicating it's the end of round one. I try to climb up on the ropes to gain height and let everyone know how wrong this setup was. We need to nail Dane to a wall, show everyone what we do with traitors. Because, for real…who in their right mind doesn't fight the honest way when facing a brother? Dane knew he had to have help to take on Calix… firing a damn bullet to pull Calix out of his element. Fucking asshole.

Except, I'm being pulled back by Dams. "Cool it,

VP. Now is not the time. Let it play out. They might have pulled this once, but he's focused now. There's no damn way he would let his gaze stray from Dane. Even if the world would end outside this ring...your ol'man wouldn't stop fighting. Let him be."

Dammit. I know Dams is right and even more... Calix told me before he got inside the ring that I was his only weakness. Oh, how I hate Dane even more in this moment, trying to gain something yet again over my damn back.

The horn blows again, time for round two. Dane barely had time to drag himself to his feet and gulp down some water that Hank is now pouring over his head. In an effort to cool him down? Or hell, make him slippery? I don't know, but the grins Beck and Bo are shooting at me from behind Dane make me even more furious than I already was. Yet all my anger fades when Calix strides toward Dane and hammers him down to the floor with one punch to the face.

Cheers erupt all around. All brothers are chanting Calix's name. Well, all except for six people. The five brothers, Ryke, Steel, Beck, Hank, and Bo, who backed Dane up. And Dane himself of course, who still hasn't regained consciousness after Calix knocked him out cold.

The horn blows three more times and right after that, my dad bellows that the fight is over. Calix won by knockout. I don't have time to go to Calix because so many men are jumping into the ring, dragging Calix out while they cheer and congratulate him. I guess he's won everyone over with kicking Dane's ass.

Well, all except for those five who are trying to drag Dane up while throwing dark looks at Calix from over their shoulders. My anger is still simmering when I step up to my father. I need to ask him what he's going to do about Dane and his buddies.

"He needs to be stripped of his patch. A brother always steps into that ring with equal value of respect. Dane needed a distraction of a fucking bullet to gain a chance of winning. He's a disgrace, he betrayed and disrespected the brotherhood. Demote that scumbag's ass," I seethe while I point at Dane who's now shaking his head in an effort to clear it. Good timing fucker, wake up because I'm going to do everything to have your ass thrown out of this club once and for all. And with this he clearly dug his own grave.

Everyone goes quiet, waiting for our Prez to answer to what I just stated. I can tell by the look on his face that he wants to agree with me, but that's just it… the reason he's Prez is because my father is the kind of man that doesn't act on impulse. He considers every angle, takes a breath and fully grasps the intention of facts, consequences, and what it all entails for the club.

"She's right," Feargal bellows. "Lack of fucking trust and that fucker pulled a knife on him too."

"Yeah," someone shouts after that and more follow, voicing their agreement.

We all know what went down but Dane's supporters are on their feet, throwing hateful glares around until Beck puts two fingers in his mouth and gives a hard whistle to quiet down the crowd.

"Let's all take a damn breath. Take it to the table for all I care but not right now. Dane is allowed to have his say but not when he just got out of this fight," Steel says in anger, trying to buy Dane time.

I want to spit some more fury their way when an arm goes around my waist, pulling me against a hard body. *Calix*. "Rein it in, firecracker. Let the Prez deal with it, you've said enough."

"Besides," Beck gloats before he adds, "we all know how women get when it concerns their ex."

I'm about to flip my shit when Calix covers my mouth with his hand, quickly whispering out his words right next to my ear. "Your ass will be sore for weeks if you don't shut up right now. Don't give them any fuel to twist this shit around."

I lean down against Calix in surrender, hating the fact that he's right. Dammit, why don't I have the kind of reason and calm in these moments like Calix and my father have? Calix's chuckle rumbles through his chest, making it vibrate through my back. He slides his hand down to my jaw and tilts my head back.

"So fucking feisty and absolutely gorgeous," he murmurs before he gives me a kiss that's over way too damn soon.

I'm still looking up, caught in a damn lust filled dream when I hear sounds of agreement ring out all around us. What the hell? I step away from Calix and punch him in the gut.

"Fucker. You did that on purpose," I snarl, angry more at myself for letting Calix turn me to mush while my father handled the issue.

"Yeah, I'm not going to apologize for that one, sweetness," Calix says on a wink. "You needed it on two grounds and you know it. Now, this issue is handled. I'm going to need a shower and a first aid kit to sew up this cut."

Shit. I step closer and grab his forearm, inspecting the cut that still has blood dripping from it. It's superficial but long enough that it needs some stitches for it to heal properly.

"Why the hell did he bring a knife into a fist fight?" I mutter to myself.

Yet another thing that's not allowed…they have to turn in any weapons because the ring is meant to hash things out with your bare hands. Seems Dane wasn't going to play fair either way. Stupid fucker because all brothers were standing around to see what he did. He might get off for the gunshot because it wasn't him that pulled the trigger, but the knife? Yeah, a nail to his own coffin.

"Come on, let's go to my room. I've got everything we need there." I grab his hand and lead him through the crowd.

Along the way, Calix gets backslaps from all the

brothers, praising him for the good fight. Some even mentioned that it was long overdue that Dane got his ass handed to him. I can't help the smile that's pinned on my face. I'm actually damn proud right now.

My father was right about Calix. He might just be the one who can turn this club around and deal with Dane once and for all. I only hope he doesn't expect me to step down. Be his ol'lady instead of a VP. Or hell, maybe he wants that title for himself...or shit... wants to take my father's place. I overheard him talking to Zack, about how he would grab the Prez patch and sow it on his pecs. Is he playing me? Playing all of us?

Dammit, why is everything complicated as fuck in life? Why can't it ever be roses and fucking sunshine, grab a bottle of wine, a book, throw your feet up and soak in the sun without worrying about anyone screwing up and putting you in the shade so dark you wonder if another sunny day will ever brighten your life?

I take a deep sigh and decide I need to think of me, my dad, this club. I can't let this man in front of me swoop me off my feet. I might have gotten carried away, he might have claimed me, and wants to see how this thing between us plays out…but that doesn't mean I've lost all my brain function. I need to be on my toes and think.

"Sit," I snap and stalk toward the bathroom.

That's about three steps. My room in the clubhouse is a tiny one. All it really has is a big bed, a desk, a TV, and a small closet where I keep some of my clothes. It's also got a tiny bathroom where my dad installed a bath. It's not much but I love it. It's a place where I can hide when I need my own space. Though I live with my father in a big house that's just five minutes away from here, it's nice to have a room all to myself too when I need it.

Not to mention we're sometimes on lockdown or have some issues we need to deal with that take up half the night and I'm too drained to get on my bike and get home. So yeah, this is a great solution.

"You're angry," Calix states.

Making me look at him as I place the first aid kid on the bed right next to him. "I'm not anything," I say and grab some gloves to snap on before getting some wipes to clean up his wound.

He says nothing and lets me. I feel his eyes on me

the whole time I'm taking care of him but I manage to focus on the task at hand. Like I said…this man is in control of himself, every situation, and if he's not he will make it so with a twist of his hands. I'm not a fool, I see a lesson in life when there is one. And right now, I need to control my emotions. *I need to get myself under control.* Meaning I also have to keep Calix at arm's length.

I've just finished putting some stitches in and bandaging up the cut when Calix puts a hand over mine. "Hey," he says in a warm and gentle tone. "What's wrong?"

"Nothing." Standing up, I grab the kit, ready to put it back into the bathroom cabinet when I hear a low growl rumble in his chest. Yeah. I should dash out of here.

"Look at me, Ten," he snaps.

I'm absolutely going to ignore that, though I keep my voice soft and steady as I tell him. "Go and head over to my father, I'm sure most of the brothers would like to talk to you."

From the corner of my eyes I see him rising from the bed. "Look. At. Me. *Tenley.*"

The way he says my name makes a shiver run through my body and I have no way of stopping my head that turns automatically toward him to connect with his intense gaze.

"That's better. Now give me the truth, what's bothering you? We will talk about it and then we'll deal with everything outside of this room. But right now, you're the one who's most important. Share, Ten. That's all I ask; open and honesty between us. That's the strength of any relationship. You're my ol'lady and a fucking VP, so we don't have the normal ol'lady shit to deal with because you will know every damn detail about club business there is to know." He crosses his inked-up arms in front of his chest but hisses when he realizes he can't due to the cut on his forearm.

His upper lip rises up in a twitching movement, frustration now plain on his face. I remember when he pulled me to him with that arm as I was about to spew more words to everyone right after Calix won. He didn't seem hurt then...yet here, in front of me, he lets me see him. All of him. Not the warrior front he throws out for everyone else. Aw shit. Here I go again, turning to mush.

"I'm frustrated, okay? *You're frustrating.* All of this is frustrating. Besides, I'm not used to having someone on my case asking me to talk about stuff. That's also very frustrating."

"Got it." The corner of his mouth twitches. "You're frustrated."

"If you're going to make fun of me, there's the damn door, asshole. I've had enough condescending bikers around me to fill me a lifetime already," I snap and instantly regret it because the look that washes over his face tells me he's about to tell me that my ass won't ever be capable of using it for sitting due to the spanking I will have to endure for mouthing off. The sad thing is…I know I'm being unreasonable. Yet I can't help myself.

"Just go and leave me alone," I sigh in a thin voice that doesn't even remotely sound like me.

CHAPTER SEVEN

CALIX

There are a lot of options going through my mind right now. One of those is the need to pull down her pants and smack that tight ass. My handprint licking her beautiful skin to a fiery red that will make my cock throb with the ache to have her. But that's not what she needs right now. I can clearly see every damn emotion that is running through her.

It's laced with a track record of history that's all wrapped in the events that happened in the last few hours. It's draining her. Add the mixture of me claiming her…hell, I'm dealing with the same damn speed she managed to collide into my life…and yet I will gladly surrender.

Except that is what's different between me and her. My life was absolute shit before she stepped into it. I had no clue what I wanted or where I was heading. Now I do because she ripped up the veil that slipped in front of my eyes. I see a future and possibilities, a damn challenge where everything is open and there to grab it with both hands. But this strong woman tip toe-ing in a biker world where every angle is scrutinized? Fuck.

Stepping forward, I take her into my arms, ignor-ing both the sting on my forearm from the cut and the way she struggles against me. I don't fucking care if she wants to be left alone, because deep down we both know that's not what she wants, *what she needs*.

After she realizes I'm not going to let her go, she gives up and sags against me. We stand there for a peaceful moment in time before I realize she's slightly shaking. Aw, fuck. She's crying and it's the kind of cry-ing where she doesn't want to and would be ashamed if I knew she was…the kind she has no control over but needs so very much right now to take some of the pressure of the turmoil of feelings that's coursing inside her.

Leaning down, I place a kiss on the top of her head while I shamelessly inhale her sweet scent. I have no clue what kind of shampoo she's using but it smells like some tropical cocktail of mango and pineapple. It reminds me of vacation, sipping smoothies down at the beach. Fuck, it's been a while since I was able to do that.

"You and me, Ten. When it's just you and me in close proximity we can totally be ourselves, okay? I would be damn grateful if you would give me your tears because I know for a fact you can't show them to anyone around here. That's gotta be tough having to deal with shit on your own, sweetness. Even if you just met me, I'm right here. I'm not a selfish bastard. I would feel grateful to share some of your burdens with you. And yeah, I damn well know I won't understand fuck about some of those issues you might have in the future but that's a guy thing, I apologize ahead of time about that stuff. Can't blame me for being a dude, you know." Oh, thank fuck. She snorts and chuckles but when she looks up I'm hit with a punch to the gut that hurts me more than the ones I endured from Dane.

"Aw, dammit, beautiful. You're breaking my heart, you know that?" I brush my lips against hers and taste the salt of her tears. Pulling back, I clear my throat, because, "Shit. See how deep you're in my system already? I adore your feistiness, the strong brat who's not taking shit from anyone, and yet you accept me where you've pushed others away. I own more damn money that I can ever spend in a lifetime, but my gut is telling me that what I'm holding in my hands might just be the most valuable thing that will ever enlighten my life."

Her eyebrows scrunch up adorably when she grumbles, "Did you just call me a brat?"

"I just mentioned I'm worth millions and you only question me calling you a brat?" I bark out a laugh and shake my head. "You're something alright." I pull her tight against me again, needing to hug her close. "Now, do you mind sharing what's gotten you so upset?"

"Everything. It's like I can't trust anyone or anything. Then there's you. My dad telling me you're the solution to our Dane problem but then you go and say shit like wanting the Prez patch and,"

"I don't want the fucking Prez patch," I interrupt

her and dammit, I should let her rant because she pokes me in the side with a finger, making me grunt but shit…I'm already sore from taking punches.

"Says you, I barely know you but you have this 'I'm serene and always in control and can totally handle myself and everything else in the process' vibe that makes me think how real you truly are. Then you go on and say other stuff and wince when you're hurting in front of me and not out there…you also swear a lot more since you met me because back in the club you were all polite and shit. You're frustrating…this is frustrating. I'm frustrated." The repeated versions of 'frustration' are thrown out on sobs so I'm back to holding her tight and letting her cry against my chest.

All of a sudden she pulls back, rubs her eyes with the back of her hand and stomps her foot. "I'm never emotional. You're killing me. Ugh. You know…sometimes I even wonder if it's all worth it. I mean, why suffer through it all? First waking up in Dane's bed months ago when I don't even have any recollection how I ended up there. Then the next morning he went out and told everyone we were together, stating he earned the VP status. Because…you know, you get that when you fuck the Prez's daughter. Getting what he wanted behind my back…then trying to get it again just now with taking you on so he's back in the running. See? *Why*? Why do I even care? My dad wanted a better future for the club, a VP who cared enough to turn shit around. Anyone who had a solid plan and was a part of the club had a chance to prove it. When I took on the challenge and brought a plan to the table, they allowed me to start and if I obtained a huge profit within a month, I had the VP patch. They fuck- ing laughed in my face when they said that. But I damn well smiled with pride when I earned that VP patch within two damn weeks. My plan was solid. None of the rest had an idea or even made an effort. I made a plan, I put it together, I made it happen, I earned that fucking VP patch with creating the car wash they all love. That earned me respect from most because I put the club first, one that I started to drag out of the gutter financially. But as long as Dane and those buddies of his are here then I'll always be just a cunt who needs to look over her shoulder. I might as well become a fuck hole because he's just waiting for me to shove me in that category once my father dies. And he will soon because my father is dying. Did you know? Did he tell you? Oh, don't look at me that way because I can see it on your face. I know more than any of these dickheads walking around the clubhouse but most will never see me as one of them. All because I have tits and a damn cunt."

I keep quiet and take my time to wait her out. Because the waterfall of words she just threw out? That non-connected, verbal throw up of emotional stress has been piling up for a long damn time.

Wait. What the hell? "What the fuck is that about ending up in Dane's bed without you having any recollection?"

She shrugs her damn shoulders. "Like I said it, I guess. I was having a drink, had maybe three glasses with two fingers worth of whiskey. I remember Dane sitting next to me the whole time. I definitely remember I was the one who initiated a kiss, and before I know it…I'm waking up the next morning in his bed while he's fucking me. There's really not much to tell."

"What the fuck, nothing to tell? You didn't get a blood test? Check and see if he used a date rape drug, anything?" I am so far off my rocker that I'm ready to tear this building apart, find Dane and skin him alive before I make his death even more painful and slow.

"No, Calix, I didn't. I got the hell out of there after I told him he could drop dead for all I care. I would be doing a happy dance on his damn grave. I was sick to my stomach and didn't leave my room after that." She groans and her cheeks turn pink from what I'm guessing is shame. "I had a crush on him at some point in time, okay? So yeah, maybe I did drink one too many and finally wanted to get over that crush since I damn well knew he's a player. Guess I got my bubble blown right in my face because in reality he was more of an asshole than I thought. The next day he told everyone we were together. I had to fight like hell to make them drop the ol'lady claim and have them believe it was a load of crap. Thankfully I had the majority behind me since they loathe Dane. So please, just let it go, I did. I got tested and to be honest? I can't remember shit. Not about that night and only very little about the next morning. It's the past, Calix. No one can change the past, you get over it and take the life lessons so you don't screw up again, or know how to avoid, or work around it. There's too much to deal with in the now to go drag out shit that happened months ago. And let's face it...then it would still be my business, not yours." She gives me a glare as a warning to shut my mouth and end this discussion.

Fat chance. The only thing I'll stay quiet about is her little admission that she had a crush on the fucker. I'll forget that little element since everyone makes mistakes in their life and I'm betting she throws it all on that angle. Talk about a pink cloud evaporating and making your ass hit the ground hard.

"One question. Does your dad know the real truth? That you can't remember shit how you ended up in his bed?" I wait for her to say something but instead she goes slightly pale.

There's my fucking answer. Dammit.

"I told you it's my business. I handled it. It's done. I gave him the crabs, okay? Well, I didn't personally. One of the girls that hangs around had it and only I knew about it, hell...she didn't even know she had it because she was complaining to me and I was the one who recognized the symptoms. Yikes, even the thought about it makes me shudder." She shudders and this actually relaxes me a hint because she's coming across as a person who doesn't let someone else throw her off. No, she has a solid damn grip on her own life, fighting for it every step of the way.

No wonder she had an emotional explosion just now. The confrontation with me and Dane, the fight, Dane fighting unfair and everyone wanting to shove things under the carpet again when it comes to this motherfucker. Yeah, she really needs a break. Not just to catch her breath from all this shit, but she needs to be pampered. Be treated like a woman who deserves heaven on Earth.

"I'm going to take you away," I tell her.

Her eyes go wide. Fuck.

"Just hear me out, okay? I was meant to catch a plane to London next week. Attend a few parties for a charity event my parents are hosting. I wasn't planning on going with this shit to deal with but I think we both need a few days away…just you and me, without all this shit."

"I can't just pack up and leave," she squeaks, her eyes almost bulging out of her head.

"Why not? I swear I will handle everything. I've

got my VP, and also C.Rash, who will move in with your father and keep an eye out. Feargal and the others will stand strong, and we'll be back within a few days. Hell, even if we only left for the weekend, that would be enough. Don't you think you deserve it? Sipping a drink in a penthouse tub, letting me take you out to dinner...come on, let's split and leave this shit for only a few days so we can recharge and face our problems head on when we get back. Next weekend. We've got one week together right here so you can make sure everything is handled. We also get to see in that week how things go at the club with the new towing business that we'll be setting up. You'll see that Dane will be out of the picture and will be waiting for us when we get back from London. Come on, take a damn moment for yourself for once. I just told you I'll handle your father and the club…meaning they can all manage without you for three damn days."

"Did I not mention that you're frustrating? Do you really think I can just pack up and leave? Even if it's for a weekend? Seriously, Dane must have hit your head harder than you thought." She shakes her head.

"Fine. Let's go." I grab her hand and take her with

me toward the door. "We're going to mention it to our Prez and let him decide."

"What? No." She tries to stop me but I'm not having any of it.

"Big Oaks!" I bellow from the hallway.

It's not Big Oaks that walks into the hallway, it's Feargal.

"Hey, Feargal, do me a favor and have Prez come see me. I need to ask him something," I tell him and he gives me a nod and disappears around the corner.

"You're insane. I can't go. Even if I have a passport, I've never even been to the west coast, let alone leave this country! I'm not going," she seethes but this time her voice is filled with panic that's clearly a whole different kind of distress.

"What's that, sweetness? Afraid to cross the ocean? Or afraid to get to know me better?" I smirk and all I get in return is a glare.

She's about to throw another tantrum when her father stalks around the corner, heading straight for us. "Calix, you wanted a word?"

"Yeah, Prez, come on in." I step inside and wait for Big Oaks and Ten to get inside before I close the door.

"You can't let this idiot put me on a plane and swoop me off for a few days vacation. Not when there's so much going on," Ten seethes, all distress is directed at her father.

Obviously, she's trying to get her father on her side, but there's one crucial mistake she's making. "Prez. Are you taking a week cool down or ten days before Dane's incident is brought to the table?"

Big Oaks is fighting a smile, I can damn well tell the man is on my side. "Ten days. I had to since I can't lynch that fucker without going through the right steps to get him kicked out for life."

"Then it would be possible to take three days, next weekend so we'll still have a week to get things started with the tow truck and see if Dane sticks to his cool down period. And for those three days, if I provide backup for you, we'd be all set, right?" I quip.

"I'm right here, you dickheads. I'm not going. You can't force me," she seethes with her eyes wide enough to let them fall out and bounce on the floor.

"I think the VP is entitled to take a few days since she got everything set businesswise. You even have this week to make sure everything is covered for this upcoming weekend. I don't have to take it to the table, that's an order, VP. You take those days because you sure as hell know all brothers can take vacation days when they've put in the work. And to speak as your father, I for damn sure think you've earned to be dragged away for some vacation days." He gives me a nod but when he turns to address his daughter, his face softens. "Come on, Cerise. Think back...when is the last time you did something for you? Or hell, took time off for that matter. You deserve this."

Cerise? The fuck? Is that an endearment he uses for her, or maybe her name...shit. That right there shows I want to know more about her. Hell, I want to know every little detail there is and even if I can have her for two or three days away from all this, just the two of us...it's what we need.

Big Oaks turns his attention toward me, shoving a finger into my pecs. "You mentioned platinum, right? Don't fuck with me, Calix. Because if I hear you've mistreated my daughter for whatever reason,"

I cut him off right there. "She's my ol'lady, Big Oaks. I already claimed her before I kicked Dane's ass. When I walked into the clubhouse and made a play at her in front of Dane it might have started out as a game to set him off, but it's not anymore, I also told her that. I'd rather slice my own throat than hurt one single hair on her gorgeous head."

Tenley has grown quiet and just eyes me and her father. What I'm about to say might freak her the fuck out or will settle her nerves somewhat. I wanted to wait some more but since the decision has already been made, I might as well get it out now.

I reach out and grab my ol'lady's hand, lacing our fingers before I tell her father, and now also my Prez. "You have the papers for my request. Zack signed off and since it was your personal invite…it's all said and done. You guys took the tow business to the table, had your vote, and with that it was agreed to have at least one brother transferred here. I'm not going anywhere as you know. I reckon we've got a week to get things started around here and have everything set to take Tenley with me to London next weekend. We'll be back within three days."

Ten tries to rip her hand from mine when my words hit but I'm not having any of that. I was expecting both explosions but I'm guessing she's still got it in her head that I'm trying to steal away the club.

"Think, Ten," I snap before I soften my voice but still make myself very clear that I'm not bullshitting here. "I'm not here to take the gavel. I'm here to push Dane out. Your father asked for my transfer to have more loyal and trusted men at his side. The tow business is an element to help the club but it was also a backdoor to get someone in without raising other questions. He wanted someone who's an outsider with a clear view on shit. That's me. Most men know me from years back so they trust me too. And yeah, I do have to admit that with you added to the mix, I don't intend to pick up and leave when this shit with Dane, and everyone else who's stirring up shit, is settled and the club can turn back to business as usual. But that's also something only you have any influence on but that's future stuff. Stuff we need to discuss and grow into. Hence the damn reason I want to take a few days where I get you all to myself so we can solidify that spark that hit us when we first met. You can't deny that, Ten. Can you? Because I'm not afraid to admit there's something deeper between us than just the need to have you."

"Take his words and the three days, Cerise, sweet-heart…your mother would want you to take a shot at something real. I can vouch for this idiot right here. I've known him since he was a punk with the tendency to go dark…from what he's lived through he took everything and turned it around. There's a reason I asked him to come here, and when Zack called me earlier… my heart might have jumped when I heard you two hit it off. Please give your father a little peace of mind… get out of this clubhouse and let yourself be pampered by a man who wants to take you on vacation. Hell, even if it's for three days or fucking pretend."

"It's not fucking pretend," I growl.

Ten pulls her hand free and I let her this time. She rubs both hands down her face and starts to mutter. "Now even my father is plain old frustrating me. When did that happen? When did everything in my life become frustrating? Do not pass go, do not collect $200. I went straight from the loony bin and into the fire pits of hell that're going to burn my ass."

Reaching out, I drag her close and whisper in her ear, "I can make sure your ass will burn, sweetness. But it will be wrapped with intense pleasure instead of the fire pits of hell."

She groans loud in frustration, making me bark out my laughter.

Ten is up to date about everything going on around here. Yet I want to talk things through with my new Prez, Big Oaks. This also gives Ten some personal time to relax. Leaving Ten in her room, we head into church and spend hours, until deep in the night to talk about everything that happened since I left here.

When I finally stalk back into Ten's room, she's already up and ready to get to work. Or hell, maybe she's avoiding me, whatever. I'm too tired to say or do anything and crash on the mattress after I kicked my boots off. I don't even have the energy to take my damn clothes off.

I wake up when it's already late in the afternoon. I take my time to freshen up and when I stroll into the main room, some brothers are already having a beer and enjoying themselves with a woman or two.

"You looking for your ol'lady?" Feargal chuckles. "She ran off on you, huh?"

I rub a hand behind my neck. "I had a long night catching up with Big Oaks, or…yeah…I guess she ran off. No use though, she'll realize that soon enough."

"She's working at the car wash. Something about needing a few days to make sure she can leave this weekend. You're taking her somewhere?" Feargal questions.

"You got that right. Good news travels fast, I hear." A smile spreads my face, knowing it was probably Big Oaks who made sure everyone knew I was taking her to London for a few days.

"When it comes to Tenley, yes. But I'm glad for the both of you, brother. I love her like a sister, she's everything you want in a wife. Come on, I'll show you so you can see for yourself." Feargal smacks me on the back and I follow him out.

When we get to the car wash, I have to refrain myself from storming to her, throwing her over my shoulder, and carrying her back to the clubhouse to spank her ass.

"What the actual fuck?" I growl.

Feargal chuckles. "Look past it, man…compare your ol'lady to the others."

I let my eyes travel over some of the other cars that are getting washed in the lot of the car wash. Guys are sitting in their cars while chicks in barely-there bikinis are washing the damn cars. Well, there's one chick who's soaping up her tits instead of the car she's standing next to, giving the customer a show I'm sure he paid big time for.

Fuck. "She's smart," I mutter.

"Oh, yeah. Why do you think she earned that VP patch? Believe me, brothers care when you bring in cash and supply entertainment while doing so. She even brought in new pussy. She's a genius I tell you. But see the difference between her and the rest who are earning their pay without guys touching them?" Feargal questions.

I shove my anger down that raised when I saw Ten in jean shorts and a lilac tank top. But seeing the rest are wearing itsy bitsy bikinis...yeah, I fucking see it.

"Ol'lady material," I agree.

"That's right. Wifey material right there...she doesn't need to show more skin to be damn sexy." Feargal's smirk leaves his face when I glare at him.

"That's my ol'lady, Feargal. Stop fucking looking," I growl and stalk over to Ten who's now hosing down the car she just washed. And she, and the damn owner of the car, should be happy the car is sitting empty.

She turns off the water when she sees me coming. "Hey," she quips.

"Don't fucking 'hey' me," I snarl, and fuck…her eyes widen and I'm probably scaring the fuck out of her and with that, I actually do a double take myself realizing I'm acting like an idiot.

"One question," I snap.

Her eyes are still wide while she nods slowly.

"Do you ever look like that?" I point at the girls with their nipples barely covered and a shoelace keeping their ass company.

"No," she snaps, her fists perched on her hips. "But what's wrong with it? Are you judging them?"

Am I? "Fuck, no. They're not my ol'lady," I state.

And that's just it…I don't want her to do it. Well, maybe if I would have my car in one of those closed garages over there where no one would see us. Understanding washes over her face at the same time I realize why my temper went through the ceiling.

"Don't get your balls in a knot. I've been making arrangements all morning to get things set for next weekend. I'm not a cheat, and I surely won't prance around and give other guys a show when I've got an ol'man, okay?" Her voice is soft and dammit... something actually settles in my chest, because she worked hard for this.

Here I stomp in and practically demand she removes herself from the very thing she build up.

I just nod, clear my throat and mutter, "Okay."

Because for real...what else is there to say? I'm in so damn deep I don't even know how to handle myself. Yet...she seems to know exactly what to say to calm my shit. There's a lot to learn, for the both of us. Good thing we've got time to work through all of this together.

CHAPTER EIGHT

TENLEY

"Why did I let you talk me into this?" I grumble. "And what the hell do I need to take with me?"

Calix's chuckle comes from the corner where my bed is. He's waiting patiently for me to pack. I, on the other hand, am not patient at all. I'm leaning toward freaking the hell out. At first, I was all frustrated when they sprang this whole vacation thing on me. But now that I had a week to think things through...yeah, I'm still not jumping with joy.

I've never been on vacation. I don't know what to expect and I was more frustrated by the idea of all of it, mainly Calix, Dane, everything. So, when my dad and Calix put me on the spot it suddenly sounded logical to step out of it all for just a few days. It's been hectic and crazy for months and all of it has been getting on my nerves.

Also, because I can't do anything about Dane and how it is now. He's been demoted, meaning he's not allowed to participate in anything club related. Hell, he's not even allowed in church. Well, not until next week when he's expected to show up when we take his situation to the table.

That's the only thing good in all of this since it gives me some piece of mind that he won't be near my father in the clubhouse. Though Calix ensures me C.Rash, Dams, and Hugo will be with my dad at all times. So that leaves me, a person who's never even left the state for more than a day or two, to get on a plane and cross the ocean.

"Don't bother with too much stuff. We will buy whatever we need in London," Calix says.

"I don't need to buy anything," I grumble. "It's just three days, all I need is my toothbrush, some toiletries, fresh panties, and a change of clothes."

"Sure," Calix says and with that I get the creepy

feeling this asshole is holding something back.

I spin around and let the bag drop in front of his feet at the same time his phone pings, indicating he's got an incoming message. His eyebrow comes up in question as to why I dumped the bag but he takes priority on the text. Fine by me, I need to grab my pills anyway. Dammit, it's a miracle I even remember to take them with me because I always screw up with taking them.

Back when I woke up in Dane's bed with him grunting above me for a blink of a moment, I was relieved when he rolled off me and snapped off the condom. At least that was one less thing to worry about, although I still got myself tested. Even if Dane demanded I'd be his ol'lady, he did nothing to give me his loyalty. Nope, openly flirting and screwing around with everything that had two legs and a cunt.

Then there's Calix. The time I've been in his presence, and that's every damn day of the last eight days he's been here, there have been many moments where other women passed by or gave him attention. Did he notice? I have no clue because he only had eyes for me. It's weird because he hasn't touched me either.

Well, the occasional heated kiss here and there, but nothing more. It's as if he's deliberately making me sexually frustrated.

I've been around bikers all my life and the only one who seemed different was my dad with my mom. All my father ever saw was my mother, true love is what my mother used to say. Hard to believe for me when they were the only example I've ever had in my life.

Strolling back, I grab my bag and shove the strip of pills in there.

"Done," I tell him.

"Packed the most crucial thing last moment, huh? Good to know you're on the pill," he says with a smirk.

"Dream on. I'm not going to screw anyone bare," I tell him, meaning every damn word.

"I haven't put my cock inside a pussy without suiting up first. I'll be sure to throw in a box of condoms as my last item on my to bring list." He reaches forward and cups my face. "Anything for you," he murmurs and brushes his lips against mine. "Let's go, sweetness. I just got a text that the plane is waiting for us."

"What?" I squeak. I mean, yeah, I was kinda expecting to get on a plane later today or tomorrow morning but I thought we needed to check when and where we could catch a flight. Not have one waiting for us, what the hell?

"Private jet, Ten. It's no big deal. One of the perks, I guess." Calix shrugs as if it's no big deal, like he just didn't mention a private freaking jet.

"I've never been on an airplane in all my life. Trust me, Calix...it is a big deal. I might totally freak out on you but that would be your fault because all of this is your insane idea. I need a drink…or hell, two." I sigh. "And London? Seriously? Why drag me off to go there when we could grab our bikes and head to a hotel for a little getaway. I know you mentioned your parents and…shit. You're not serious about attending parties or visiting your parents, right? Oh, Christ, tell me you're kidding."

"We're going, Ten. And why the fuck would you mind meeting my mother when I've already met your father?" he growls in my face as if I've offended him. And why does he only mention his mom when he was talking about his parents earlier…why not mention his dad too?

"Yeah, well…my dad happens to be your Prez now

too, so that's irrelevant," I growl right back.

"You're just looking for something to throw at me, go on pretty girl...throw some more, it won't make a lick of difference. We're going and that's final," he snaps.

"Well, if you think I'm going to wear a gala dress and throw makeup on, you're sadly mistaken," I snap back.

His head tips back and laughter escapes. When he connects his gaze with mine, amusement is written all over his face. "Oh, sweetness, I don't care about any of it. You're perfect the way you are. Besides, I've been wearing suits all my life except for when I'm in my club. It's only recent that I've inked my hands and neck and threw the suits in the closet. I'm pretty sure all eyes will be on me when we walk into parties and I will stick out like a sore thumb. I'll be honored to have you walking right next to me because you're the most gorgeous woman no matter what you're wearing, makeup or not, I don't care about any of it...only you, the rest of this world is irrelevant."

Dammit, here I go, swooning over this guy again. "Keep talking like that and I'll only wear my crotchless panties."

His eyes flare and his fingers wrap around my throat, pulling me close. "I fucking dare you." His breath tickles my lips and makes a wave of longing to have him run through my body.

"Dammit. I don't own a pair, I was just thinking out loud. But I could definitely buy a pair, they'd have to be purple, though. If I'm wearing nothing else, they'd have to match my hair." I'm rambling but he's staring at me so intently that my mind is just bouncing around, waving for attention.

And I need it. Attention. Mainly for the place between my legs. The way he's primed my body for days and days without giving me any release. Even when we shared a bed he still didn't touch me. He only pulled me close, being the perfect gentlemen, falling asleep in each other's arms.

"Purple is good," he whispers and slowly closes the distance until our lips meet.

Slow. Sensual. Yet he catches me in a kiss as if he's searching for my soul to claim his ground, forcing a merge that will bind me to him forever. Both his hands are guiding my head, holding me as if I'm his most precious possession. I want to open my eyes to know that I'm not dreaming but I just can't. This man has the ability to make me float on his adoration, to feel as if we're the only two people alive without needing anything else.

His phone starts to ring and I've got the serious need to grab that thing and slam it into a wall, hating the fact that we got interrupted. Shit. Calix was right. A few days away, just the two of us, might be what I need. To see if there's something else besides him being able to swoop me off my feet. Open myself up to find out if this ol'lady thing is really a partnership. And yet only the future will be able to tell because he now belongs to this MC.

Meaning I'm officially his VP. This powerful, contained, graceful, and controlling man...*my ol'man*... would have to follow my orders. There hasn't been a dilemma or situation where it was needed this week, but it's bound to happen that I need to step in and then he would have to follow my orders.

That to think I've pulled him out of a BDSM club, a Dom. Taking orders from me, and yet the way he kissed me just now? Gah, why is life so freaking hard and confusing? Why are there labels, rules, and most of all standards we need to live up to? All of that complicates the shit out of life.

I just want a man who treats me like a partner, an equal. One who lifts me up and supports me when I need it. One who's freaking good in bed and yeah, that muscle, ink, and handsomeness Calix is sporting is on my 'perfect man' list too. So, here's to hoping and giving a shot at something I want in life. First though... I need to get my ass on a plane. Most definitely not something I look forward to.

Calix slows our kiss and rubs his thumb over my bottom lip before stepping away to take the call. I take this time to catch my breath. Dammit, this man is consuming. Okay, think. Is there anything else I should bring? What should I bring? This is probably the reason why I never went on vacation. This is pure stress. The hell with relaxing. I've got everything I need right here, why leave?

"We're on our way, be there in forty minutes, tops," Calix says and ends the call. He gives me a reassuring smile, as if he knows my mind is on the run again. "Time to go, Ten. Like I said, if we need anything else, we'll get it when we get there."

All I give in return is a nod and grab my backpack that's got my passport, and everything else I think I need. Here goes nothing, right?

My dad, Hugo, Dams, C.Rash, Feargal, and a few others walk us out. Calix said we should only take one bike to the airport and that it should be his. Though he might be right, I bet it was because he wanted me on the back of his. Strangely this is the first time I've ever done this. Well, I did ride with my father when I was young, but as soon as I was able to, I bought my own.

It's strange. *The good kind of strange*. Holding on, trusting another person and just relishing in the feel of the bike and the wind, guiding you over the road your partner chooses for the both of you. Yeah, I clearly think too much. I need to drop everything and slip into vacation mode. Enjoy. Have freaking fun and don't overthink.

But I guess I overdid the 'have freaking fun and don't overthink' because I don't remember much about the flight or getting to the hotel. It's all a blur and I swear I won't ever drink again. That's also what happened with Dane. I drank three whiskeys and they were only two fingers high each. Alcohol isn't for me, that's for sure. Two or four beers, yes, all good. But no more whiskey or champagne for that matter.

The huge difference between Dane and Calix... waking up after having too much to drink...is that now, I'm still fully dressed, lying on top of the sheets while Calix is staring down on me.

There's a frown above his eyes. "Is this what happens every time you have a drink?"

I try to sit up but my head is starting to pound. I close my eyes and rub my forehead. "Not with beer... whiskey, and now I know champagne has the same effect. So that's a yes. I have no clue about other stuff since I've only tried that. Normally I keep it to a beer or two."

"No more alcohol for you," he simply states.

"Brilliant conclusion, smartass. I just came to the same realization," I mutter but when I open my eyes I realize I should have rephrased it a bit.

"You're damn lucky you're hurting right now otherwise your ass would be wearing my handprint." A muscle in his jaw ticks and even if his voice is calm and collected, it's the promise in there that makes me shiver.

Oh, yeah...I'm actually regretting the fact that I drank champagne during our flight where I could have joined the mile-high club instead. Dammit. We've had so many moments where we could have screwed each other's brains out and yet every time there's something that prevents it from happening. Like now. Ugh. It seems like Calix has enough restraint for the both of us.

"I need a shower. And food. Definitely food. After that my ass is all yours," I grumble and scoot off the bed to head for the bathroom but my path is blocked.

"Be very careful with those kinds of promises, Tenley. I might come across as a person who's got a good grip on himself but I do have my limits." His voice is dark and raw, as if I just said something that pissed him off and turned him on simultaneously.

Dammit. I bet it's the same thing that went through my head too. "I'm going to mention his name once and then we'll be done with it. I get it, that's probably the same thing that happened when I had whiskey and ended up in Dane's bed. See why I didn't say anything? It happened. I had a crush, he turned out to be an asshole, I got over it. So there, discussion closed. I agree with you, no more alcohol for me."

"It still shouldn't have happened. Fucking is both parties present with a clear head. He's more than an asshole, he's,"

My hands fly up to cup his face. "Irrelevant. That's what he is. Like I said, we're going to be done with it. You mentioned something about getting to know each other? So that's what we'll be doing these next few days, instead of talking about others, okay?"

I can tell he's torn and this makes me actually smile because it shows he can't let go, that it's something he struggles with. And I totally get it because what happened didn't benefit the ongoing shit that Dane brought to the club. The way Dane forces himself into a position he claims is his to take, *the VP status*. Trying to take me his ol'lady, trying to get my father into an early grave to become president…the Dane shit-list is long.

He steps away and shakes his head. "Go, grab a shower. I need to make a few calls and then I'll take you out for some breakfast, okay?"

Breakfast. Dammit. I slept for hours. We left last

night and then with the time difference gained a few hours, but it seems I've slept through all of it and woke up Saturday morning. Great. Maybe I need to do this when we get back, it does speed things up, that's for sure.

Crossing the large bedroom, I make my way into the bathroom and it's then I realize what a massive suite we have. Insane actually. Even the bathroom is three times as large as my room back at the clubhouse. The tiles are all a fresh light blue on the left wall and there's a tub in the center. Like really in the middle of the space with nothing around it. There's a shower with glass walls around it in the corner and mirrors with a counter on the left of it.

Suddenly I feel like taking a quick shower isn't something I need. What I would like is to sit in that tub and stare around me for a long time while soaking in hot water. And that's exactly what I'm going to do.

The sound of running water is the only thing I'm hearing while I strip out of my clothes. I'm sure Calix is making phone calls like he said and this suite being large indicates he's either stepped into another room or is very quiet. Either way, that's not my concern.

Relaxing is. It doesn't take long for my ass to be deep into the comfort of hot water. My fingers are a show and tell of how long I've been soaking.

Calix strolls in and holds out a large towel. "Come on, sweetness, time to get out and have some breakfast. And I've also had some dresses and other stuff delivered that I hope you will pick one from to wear tonight." The corner of his mouth twitches. "If you haven't changed your mind about wearing only crotchless panties, then we need to go shopping first."

"Meeting the parents, right? I'm going to need panties for that one," I grumble while taking the towel and start to dry myself off.

Then I realize that I don't even know a thing about his background, nor his parents.

"What's the party we're attending? And will both your parents be there? Can you tell me a little about them? About you?" Woah. Question tornado. Stupid me, I should have spread that out a bit.

Calix's mouth turns into a flat line. "I think it's better when you get to meet them first without me giving you the rundown. I've already let my mother know I'll be attending one event and that's it."

"Jeeezzz, Calix, that sounds reassuring." I roll my eyes, put the towel over the rack and stroll into the bedroom to grab some underwear but come to a stop when I notice a rack filled with gorgeous dresses.

But there's one that catches my attention immediately. It's a stunning, deep purple gown with a long split to show some leg. The body is form fitting bodice and an illusion sweetheart neckline. Completing the look is bead embellished lace that flows over the shoulder and down the back. Delicate, graceful, and something I would never dreamed of buying, let alone wearing.

I want to dive into my bag to grab some underwear but there's a tiny bag on the bed where a hint of purple catches my eye. Rushing over, I rip out the lace bra and thong that would go perfectly underneath the dress.

Spinning around, I jump straight into Calix's arms. No words of appreciation are needed when I kiss him fiercely and wrap my legs around him, letting him know with my whole body how insanely happy I am with his choice of clothes for me to wear tonight.

CHAPTER NINE

CALIX

A bare ass in my hands, her tongue down my throat, and a set of damn fine breasts pressing against me. Nothing. Not one goddamn thing will keep me from getting inside her. We've been waiting and dancing around it too long already.

She groans into my mouth and realizes the shift in the air around us, it's now loaded with the need to have one another. Yet I don't want to rush into it, bury myself deep, pound until we both blow. Fuck no. That's something that's still spiking the dominate side in me. The need to control things, delay so every second is well spent. Learning her body and with that making sure to give her the kind of pleasure she deserves.

My woman comes first. Always. With anything in life and it's a feeling that settles deep inside me to know that she is the one for me. A brat who's got enough fire inside her to see through me, when to call it out and when to let it slide. Like she handled the fact that I didn't want to talk about my parents. Just gave me a bratty response and walked away.

I wouldn't ever let anyone walk away like that before I met her. But with her? I take everything she throws at me. Yeah, up to a certain level of course, but still...I itch to have her stand up to me, it spikes something that's rooted in my bones. A fire only she creates and knows how to tame and handle.

Like now, swirling her tongue around mine, sucking it slowly as if she wants me to feel what it would be like when she'd have my cock between those fuckable lips of hers. I walk to the bed and lean over so I can slowly place her on the bed. Glancing down, she stays in the exact same position I laid her down in. Knees falling open, pussy on show for me, and her hair spread like a wild mess around her.

"Damn gorgeous," I whisper, more to myself than

to her.

She is the most stunning woman in an explosive package. Unique. The key element I was missing in my life. The excitement she brings, the challenge, the chance to have a future together.

Her legs tremble, threatening to close. Placing a hand on each knee to keep them in place, I intone. "Let me enjoy the view, sweetness. You have no idea how bad I want you right now. To claim what truly belongs to me. To make you mine in the way you give your-self to me, fully, openly. The most precious of gifts I've never been more honored to receive." My damn voice cracks from the emotion that's laying heavy on my heart. And with it shows that this isn't just a fuck to get off. No, this is way more than that.

"Are you ready, Ten? Because I will tell you right now that when I have you, there's no going back. It will be you and me. When my cock enters this," I let my fingers slide through her pussy that's already soaked from excitement, prepared to welcome my cock. "You'll be mine. Understood?"

"Yours," she groans and moves her hips to seek pressure from my hand to get herself off.

Pulling back, I give her an open hand smack on her pussy.

"Don't rush things, Ten. I'm in control when we're having sex, unless I demand otherwise. I'll be the one who will give you pleasure and determine when it's time for you to welcome the orgasm I will give. Is that clear?"

"Clear," she moans and willingly lets her legs fall all the way open.

An invite. A submission. Surrendering herself to me, trusting that I will give her the exact things I promised her. One I don't take lightly and one I fucking damn well never thought I'd have for myself. I've never claimed a woman like this. The thought is overwhelming, the need to possess, to own, to claim. "*Mine*," I growl low.

I step away for one final time to grab a condom and throw it on the mattress beside her. Stripping away all my clothes, the final barrier between us, I place a knee on the bed and hover over her. She reaches up with her pelvis, searching for my cock to fill her up. I grab her hip and push her down into the mattress. Before she can do anything else, I take a nipple into my mouth and swirl my tongue around it. Her fingers run through my hair, keeping me close. *I'm not going anywhere, love.*

She's caged underneath me and it would be so easy to throw my hips forward and slide right into her tight hot pussy, but I won't. Not yet. She's ready for it, I can feel her heat, smell her arousal, hear the little sounds she makes, and sense the way she writhes underneath me. It's empowering to become aware how badly we want each other, to share the same craving and need.

Latching onto her other breast, I take the tight peak between my teeth and bite down at the same moment I let my bare cock press down over her clit. Rocking forward to create friction and fuck...she lights up beautifully, screaming my name while her nails press down into my scalp.

"Oh, God...oh, God...that's...you're...I need more," she rasps out between breaths.

"And you'll get more," I vow, moving down to nestle myself between her legs.

I run my thumbs up and down her slit. Soaked. Puffy. Ready for my cock. But not yet. I need to taste her, make her come on my tongue before she will light up from taking my cock deep inside her.

"Look at that. This pleases me very much, sweetness. All slick and glistening. I'm going to put my mouth on you but I want you to grab my head, you know why?"

She shakes her head furiously, biting her bottom lip while eying me so lustful I want to jump in and fuck her raw because that's what her eyes are demanding of me.

"I want your hands on me. Because I for damn sure won't hold back. Meaning I will take that bundle of nerves between my teeth and nibble on it, maybe a little too rough and this is where you will come in. Pull me closer if you need more or yank my hair if you can't take anymore. Fair warning, though...I won't fucking care, and I won't stop. Whatever you can or can't take, that's for me to decide. Am I making myself clear? I won't stop till I've sucked the pleasure straight from the source."

Ever so slowly, I move down and hover just above her wet pussy. Releasing a hot breath, I relish in the fact that she shivers beneath me. That's what I'm talking about. The buildup. She already came once but is craving her next fix with such longing and anticipation, it will only enhance the pleasure I'm determined to give her.

Lazily, I lick from ass to clit, digging my fingers into her hips so she's prevented from shooting up. I'm a starving man who's just found the only food left on the planet. She tastes like the pleasure I just gave her, but I need more.

Closing my mouth around her clit, I start to suck and flip that bundle, giving it my full attention. Ten starts to moan and tries to pull me off. Yeah, I warned her, didn't I? She can take it, she has to. It's already so sensitive and responsive since she just came a moment ago. *But I'll give her so much more.*

When I finally bury myself deep, she will feel every inch a thousand times over. She will never forget our first time together. The way I give her my full attention, every element of her body will be pleasured. Even her damn mind.

And that's exactly it. She's not closing her eyes or throwing her head back…she's got her gaze pinned on me, watching my every move as if she can't believe this is truly happening. Same here, love…same here.

It's damn magical to find the one person that you can connect with on so many levels.

I shake my head to rub her sensitive flesh with my scruff. She gasps while I relish in the way her taste intensifies. She's already so close. Hell, even my cock is so painfully hard right now that it takes everything I've got to keep my mouth sucking her clit, instead of surging inside her so I can come with her. I slide two fingers into her sweet pussy without warning, making her tip over into a sea of pleasure.

Her pussy ripples around my fingers, my name spilling from her lips as she moans freely. Fuck. I love how she holds nothing back. Hell…I bet three doors down they heard her screaming with pleasure. That fucking loud.

Leaning back, I lick my fingers and reach for the condom. Ripping the package with my teeth, I palm my cock and give it a good squeeze before rolling it on. Lining myself up to enter her, but before I do, I surprise her by tapping her clit a few times with the head of my cock, making her squeal.

"I'm going to go slow but you're tight, sweetness." I hiss through my teeth when I push the head inside her as she greedily starts to take me. Fuck me, that feels good.

I should give her time to accommodate me but I simply can't. She feels so damn right. One hard thrust and I'm balls deep. And with that I might have scratch marks along with all the scars on my back, but it's totally worth it.

"Just wait, love. Your pussy was made to welcome me inside…it's been waiting forever but the wait is over now. I won't ever get enough." Sliding out slowly, I take my time to guide right back in. She's so slick that it heightens everything because her pussy feels like a damn tight fist that's gripping me like it won't ever let me leave. "Fuck…you're heaven," I groan, picking up speed.

I hook her leg over my elbow, opening her up to fuck her hard and deep. I can't hold back. I feel like a mad man who needs to make sure this pussy knows just what cock it belongs to. Sweat is running down my back, my pelvis hitting her with force and yet she groans to give her more. *She's fucking perfect.*

I'm most definitely a goner when it comes to her. I wanted to drag this out and yet in reality I'm already chasing my own damn orgasm because if it doesn't hit soon I'll go insane. Tilting my hips, I make sure to hit her clit with every pump forward and that's when her eyes roll into the back of her head.

For the third time my name is bouncing off the walls but this time, I bellow out hers right after it. Grunting, I lazily keep pumping inside her until I'm sure there's nothing more to give. I crash down on top of her, giving her my full weight because there's no more energy left inside me. Instead of complaining, she hugs me tight.

We're both out of breath and trying to calm our racing hearts. Mine is beating just as fast as hers. I feel wetness trickling out and that makes me aware of the fact that I need to clean up. Regretfully, I drag myself up and pull out. Seeing, and realizing what happened.

"You're on the pill, right, Tenley?" Fuck.

Ten raises up and glances down. She keeps staring at my cock that's covered with a condom except the thing tore straight through. I knew I never fucked another woman so damn hard, and this is the result.

"We would have fucked bare in the first place if the choice was up to me. I'm clean, always used a rubber and this," I point down while I rip off the shredded condom, "hasn't happened ever before. Clearly you bring out the best in me," I tell her with a smirk and yet she still keeps staring at me without saying anything.

I have a weird feeling about her reaction but I need to take care of the condom first. I stalk into the bathroom to throw it into the trash and grab a washcloth, making it wet with warm water before I return to the bedroom.

Ten is staring up at the ceiling, her body still in the same pose as I left her. I nestle myself back between her legs to clean her up, except she jolts up as if she just now realizes she's not alone.

"What the hell are you doing?" she gasps and bats my hand away.

"Cleaning you up. Lay back and let me or I'll flip you over, smack your ass, and still clean you up," I growl.

I'm getting a bit pissed and don't understand why she's acting this way after we just had hot, dirty, mighty-fucking-fine sex. Yes, I understand the seriousness of a condom tearing, and the damn consequences. Even if there's little chance, I will always step up and be there.

Hell, with the kind of father and upbringing I've had? I never thought about having children, let alone finding a woman I wanted to share the rest of my life with. Mainly because I was career driven, always busy and no time for commitment, but for fuck's sake…I've never met the right woman. I have now, because with the brilliant woman in front of me, I want all of it. And with that knowledge…I'm not freaking out…but she is.

She obliges. Gently I clean her up and put the washcloth over the rack. When I've crawled into the bed with her, I pull her close, thankful she lets me without any fuss. With her finger she starts to trace the ink on my abs.

"I'm not good with my pill…I mean, I forget all the time." She sighs. "I'm stupid like that but it's not like I have a relationship or fuck all the time. Hell, I've never had a boyfriend because with the club you're either an ol'lady or you're one who bounces around from dick to dick. I'm neither."

"You *are* one now, *an ol'lady*. You're mine," I growl again. Fucking hell, my temper has done a one eighty since I met this woman. I was all calm and collected yet when I'm around her I turn all brainless caveman for no fucking reason.

"I know that, you big growly teddy bear. I was just saying that we need to be careful. Seems like no matter how safe you are, precautions taken…there's always a possibility that life throws you a curve, right? I'll google a pharmacist, get a morning after pill."

"I'm not a growly teddy bear, and you're not taking a morning after pill," I growl. "Fuck. I am a growly teddy bear," I mutter.

She laughs and straddles me. "You are, and I am. We can't take the risk."

"I vote we wait it out. The chance is minor, no need to take any meds to screw with your body. Hey…if you wiggle that tight ass again over my cock, I'll fuck you bare and double my chances to knock you up." I mention it as a joke but once the words are out, they sound damn fine to me.

"No, no. We need to put two condoms on that big dick of yours. Or didn't you get the max size or something? Is that the reason it ripped?" She leans forward and licks my damn nipple, making the skin wet and fucking tickle.

My hands go to her waist, pressing her down on my cock that hardened beneath her. "Wearing two condoms is risky, the added friction will make it tear, so no...not gonna happen. Why not fuck bare? No barrier between us. And it wasn't the condom's fault we ripped it, Ten. It was the hard, raw, full power fucking we did."

She groans from the way I rotate my hips, making sure my cock is burning hot against her core without entering. Sliding my hand up her back, I bury my fist into her hair and pull her head up.

"You're mine. I can take care of you for a lifetime, even if we have triplets. Wanna fuck bare? I do. I'm all in. You?" I take away her chance to reply, dragging her down for a hard kiss before I pull her back to add. "No damn pressure because I've got a box of condoms. I'll put one on if you want, we'll fuck nice and slow. The choice is yours."

I'm really screwed up in the head because I'm hoping she ditches the pills and we throw away the condoms, because if I knock her up...we'll be connected through blood. My chest tightens with the thought and with this I know for sure she's it for me. My forever girl. I'm not letting go. I'll fucking fight or die for her if I have to. So, any choice she makes, I'll stand right beside her.

"Hmmm," she moans. "You've got to stop rubbing me like that. No fair, it takes away all my options to think."

Fucking perfect. More cock distraction...coming up. I make sure to keep grinding while I bring our mouths together again. She surprises the fuck out of me when she reaches between our bodies, grabs my cock and takes me inside her.

"Fuuuuuuuuuck," I groan.

My eyes roll into the back of my head. Damn that feels so fucking perfect. No damn rubber barrier. I feel all of her. Hot. Tight. The head of my cock is buried so fucking deep in this position I don't think it's ever been buried in something that feels so damn good.

Instead of bouncing on my cock, Ten just starts to rock her hips, grinding, rotating, hell if I know what those magic moves are but she needs to keep it up.

"So good," I murmur. Yeah, I have nothing epic to say because the epic-ness is all her, that's for fucking sure.

CHAPTER TEN

TENLEY

Oh, man…Hello, my name is Tenley Cerise Oaks, I'm horny as hell and an addict when it comes to this man's magnificent cock. Holy shit, there's nothing that compares to him. The way he handles himself, the way he is; *it's everything*. I could easily see myself falling for this guy. Ugh…who am I kidding? I'm already on the path of adoration, heading toward the big mountain of love.

I grind myself against him, over and over. His hands are on my hips, holding me tight while he pushes himself off the mattress to surge even deeper inside me. I can't hold back. He fills me up completely, hitting just the right spot inside me while managing to stroke my clit with every move. Tipping my head back, I release a scream of pleasure while I let the orgasm overtake me.

Calix curses and then I feel him come inside me. Hot jets. I've never let anyone come inside me and I must say it's so freaking different than having sex with the use of a condom. Not to mention the feel of his cock pulsing, emptying himself deep within me. It's as if it's more complete, holding nothing back while we give each other everything there is to give and more.

"I think I'm going to sleep right here," I mutter and make myself comfortable on his chest.

Well, actually, I just flopped my hands out from underneath me and closed my eyes. I could totally take a nap. A long one. All my energy is gone. Holy shit. That's a first. The only experience I've had was missionary position and that takes very little effort and not a lot of options to participate in a way Calix let me. Or what he did. Whatever. I push the thought away because all I need is what I have now. Releasing a deep sigh, I let myself drift off while being in the comfort of his embrace.

My nap is cut short when Calix softly rolls over, allowing him the space to get up. "You awake, sweetness? Did you want to order room service, or will you let me take you out to grab something to eat? We've got about three hours before we have to get ready for the party."

Three hours…I check my phone and see that it's already late. "We've slept that long?" I squeak.

"You needed it, and to be honest…I didn't mind holding your naked body tight against me and I would have enjoyed it even longer, but I have one social duty and then I'm off the hook till next year." Calix gives me a tiny smile before he reaches for his suit.

Suit? Holy hell. Shamelessly I watch how this muscled, inked up man merges himself with a white suit. Breathtaking, like it's made specially for him. Dammit, I don't think I've ever seen anyone look this captivating and in tuned with himself.

"Get dressed, Tenley. I'm not going to take that pussy again until after the party," he tells me with a strained voice.

"Nice. So if I'm good, I'll get a treat, huh?" I roll my eyes and slip off the bed.

Calix adjusts his dick that's tenting his slacks. "I think it's me who's getting the treat when this night is over. It'll be a miracle if I can contain myself around that fucker this time. Though that fucker is going to have a contained fit once he sees the ink on my hands and neck."

A contained fit? That fucker? What the hell is he talking about, and why does he have that look on his face? It's as if he's angry, nervous, and anxious all at once.

"Your father?" I'm guessing here, although it's not that hard to guess.

A muscle in his jaw ticks. "Yes."

He doesn't elaborate and with us needing to get something to eat and get ready for the party, I'm positive I won't get a word out of him about this right now.

"Okay. Sex after the party and then we'll have a long talk. You wanted this weekend to get to know each other, you start to spill when we've handled all of this. Deal?"

"Spill as in my cum inside your pussy?" He freaking smirks and I'm debating smacking or kissing it off his damn face.

"Whatever," I grumble and start to get dressed.

We choose to grab a bite to eat at some fancy restaurant Calix picked. I actually like it because I'm so out of my element it's good to have some sort of trial run before I have to go inside a ballroom. Calix explained how these parties go. At first, I was nervous and yet knowing he's right beside me, I feel like I could face anything.

It's also made it very clear to me that Calix would be able to handle a lot of things. Some might say he's got different faces, a mask, never showing the real him but personalities he slips into…a detective, a biker, a bartender, a freaking Dom. How wrong they would be. In the short time I've known him, there's one thing very clear. *He's all of it.*

There is no act or mask. If I'd have to pick anyone who would have all the abilities to rule a country, it would be him. He's got the strength and the knowledge to handle anything and I'll gladly follow him. Though with knowing and realizing all of this…I can also see a hint of his pain. A struggle. Something he hides deep and doesn't show and yet I see it. It's in his eyes, the small line that slides in even though he hides it pretty well.

We just got back from dinner and changed into the perfect clothes for this charity. I'm loving my purple dress. It feels like a second skin that flows around me so freaking gorgeous with every step I take. Calix ordered the complete outfit, from the dress to the underwear, and the perfect strappy heels along with it. I've styled my hair, let it hang loose so it's slightly curly.

"You're stunning, Ten. Stop fidgeting." Calix chuckles and places a hand at the small of my back, guiding me onto a carpet that guides us toward the entrance.

Camera flashes are everywhere and this is something Calix also mentioned. The one time a year he attends charity parties is to indulge his parents, show his face enough to keep them happy until next year.

"And you should smile instead of looking grumpy," I tell him.

A photographer is shouting Calix's name. Calix turns and pulls me closer, taking a moment to pose for the camera. I can't help but place a hand on his chest while looking at his beautiful face that's now got a seductive smile he's directing right at me. My heart beats faster and I'm tempted to get on my toes and kiss the hell out of him.

Calix chuckles as if he knows exactly what I'm thinking. Instead of pulling away, he decides to give everyone a little show when he leans in and kisses me fiercely. For a moment I think we're about to take it to the next level but thankfully Calix pulls back and brushes his nose gently against mine.

"So damn tempting." His voice is loaded with emotion.

"Let's get this party over with," I croak.

"My thoughts exactly," Calix growls and guides me inside.

In this moment, I feel like a princess. A princess who's been swept off her feet by a prince who is willing to give her everything she needs. And this has nothing to do with the massive ballroom I'm standing in, the expensive dress I'm wearing, or how much money Calix has in his bank account. We could be naked and living in a dump for all I care. It's him. It's us. It's the way he handles himself, and me.

He makes me want to be a better person. Think through steps to make the right choice and grab hold once I've made a decision. In a short period of time he's shown me that he has my back, wants to have a future with me and has dragged me off to meet his parents and the world that's woven into his background.

"I see my parents. All the way in the back on the left," Calix murmurs into my ear as we move through the large space.

Though it's a large room, it's very crowded. People beautifully dressed, women in all kinds of formal dresses, men with black suits. Inside I'm smiling huge because not only does Calix stand out in his white suit…he's also the only one who's got ink creeping out underneath his suit.

Yet he fits in with his grace, finesse, perfect suit, and manners. He makes me feel ten inches taller just being here with him. Leaning in some more, I whisper, "I adore your hot ass."

Okay. That came out a little different than it sounded in my head.

Calix comes to a stop and chuckles. "Just my ass, sweetness?"

I groan and roll my eyes. "No, silly. Not just your ass, although that is freaking perfect. I wanted to say

I adore you. *All of you*."

"That's a very nice thing to say, miss. Calix, will you please introduce me to your guest?" a woman's voice interrupts us.

I'm captivated by the way Calix's face fills with love and warmth for this woman. If I thought he was handsome in all the ways he was around me? He's absolutely breathtaking now.

"Mother." He leans in and kisses her cheek, briefly gives her a hug before stepping back. "May I introduce Tenley. My future wife."

Oh. My. Personal. Hell. On. Earth. I'm sure my cheeks are flaming red. But no one will notice because I'm suddenly pulled into a tight hug by Calix's mom. And judging by her shaking and the wetness I feel on my shoulder...I swear she's crying.

"Aw, ma...give her a little room to breathe and I'm sure father will flip if he sees you've ruined your makeup," Calix groans.

The woman releases me, steps back but just as quickly cups my face. "Oh, look at you. You're so beautiful." Her eyes meet Calix. "You've done very well for yourself son. She's breathtaking."

She gives me another smile through teary eyes before she hugs Calix and excuses herself to go to the bathroom to make herself presentable again.

"Fuck. Here it comes," Calix mumbles and I don't even have time to look at him to see what he means before I hear a very harsh voice.

"What did you do now, Calix? Why is your mother leaving our guests?" The man in the black suit might look pristine but there's an underlying cruelty simmering in his eyes that gives me the chills. He leans closer to Calix, keeps his voice low and yet I pick up on it. "And let's forget about the disgusting way you've mutilated your skin for all to see."

What the hell? It's the devil in disguise. I can't state it any other way.

"That would be my fault, seeing your wife was ecstatic to know her son is getting married so she was overwhelmed with joy...for us," I quip and lean against Calix who's turned to stone.

The man looks at me as if he's running me through a quick CT scan.

Reaching out, I attempt to break the frost that has settled in around us. "Hello, I'm Tenley Cerise Oaks.

Please to meet you, sir."

He stretches out and takes my hand. They say you can tell a lot about a person from their handshake and yet this one freaks me out. I don't like the softy shake because my own is firm and this makes him tighten his hold on my hand. This man is either trying to intimidate me or he thinks this is the start of an arm wrestling match because my fingers are getting squished. Whatever. I don't give one freaking bleep but plaster a smile in place instead.

"What do you do for a living, Tenley? Or have you put your hooks into our family name so you can,"

"I co-own a company in the automotive industry, sir. And only recently I've started up a car wash to branch out. With only a few months into it, it's turned out very profitable. So, you might say Calix put his hooks in me, not the other way around." I give him a wink and a warm smile while in the meantime I would like to throat punch the man and poke my fingers into his eyes. Twice in case I don't shove them hard enough the first time.

"A business woman. That's somewhat admirable, I guess," the man says in a condescending tone.

Calix's mom returns and the man in front of me morphs into a perfect gentleman, taking his wife's hand, kissing it before pulling her close. "Eliza, there you are. I hear you've met Calix's fiancée already."

"Yes," Eliza gushes. "I can't believe the day has come that our son is finally settling down."

All this time, I'm holding a statue. Anger is radiating off Calix and the way his fists are clenching is a show and tell he would like nothing more than to kick his father's ass and show him every corner of this ballroom. Somehow the thought hits me that the reason he doesn't act on it is because of his mother.

How can this woman not see what kind of person this man is? Or...hell. For real? Would Calix's father be someone who will only become vicious when his wife's back is turned? Why? Why would you do that? I take a close look at Calix's father and the way his eyes light up when he looks at his wife is in utter adoration. I get the feeling that this woman just might be the only living soul on earth this man respects. Fucker.

"Better believe it," Calix says and I can tell he's putting in the effort to make it sound nice.

"I'll believe it when we get the invitation to the

wedding," Calix's father states with a hard voice.

I would like to kick this man off the damn throne he thinks he's sitting on. Who the hell does he think he is talking to his son like that? But most of all? I think there's more to it than that because the hatred Calix has for this man is rolling off him in waves. Not to mention the fact that Calix didn't want to talk about it beforehand.

Makes sense because I think I would be tempted to punch him on sight. Smart thinking on Calix's part. But I'm not related so I can shock this man, sneer right back or whatever I feel like doing.

"We might not invite anyone and go for a quick Vegas wedding." I look up at Calix just in time to see the corner of his mouth twitch in amusement.

Calix's mother gasps. "Oh, you wouldn't dare take my only son's wedding away from me."

Shit. My mind is running to think of something to say but I don't have to because Calix seems to jump on the 'let's shock the parents boat too. "Tenley is only speeding things up, mother. Since I might have gotten a little excited after she said yes…enough to make a condom snap straight through the middle."

"Calix," his father scolds while his mother's eyes flare in shock.

"Oh. You're not kidding me, are you, son? Please." Calix's mother turns to me. "Tell me he's not kidding. Are you two starting a family? So soon?"

"Did you knock her up? Did she punch a hole in the condom to bind your fortune to her?" Calix's father's true colors start to shine through…maybe his mother does know what kind of person her husband really is.

"Henry," Calix's mother scolds. "Be civil."

Henry nods and gives her a muttered apology, but his regret doesn't last long.

Calix chuckles and gives me a kiss on the top of my head. "I hope I knocked her up, but since I just took her mere hours ago we won't know for sure until at least a few weeks from now."

Henry tenses and his face is starting to turn red. As if he's reaching boiling point and can blow at any time. Eliza places her hand on Henry's chest. Raising on her tiptoes she kisses his cheek and whispers something in his ear. Tension visibly drains his body.

Eliza turns to us. "Come on you two. Let me introduce you to a few of the guests."

We let her lead us away from Henry and around the ballroom, stopping here and there to shake hands and have some small talk with people I have no clue who they are and will most likely never meet again.

A guy stalks toward us and shakes Calix's hand. It looks like they're old friends the way Calix openly smacks the guy's shoulder and gives him a warm greeting. I'm caught staring at the two when Calix reaches over and pulls me close.

"Jag. Let me introduce you to my fiancé, Tenley," Calix says with a grin and I must say, it's infectious.

At first, I thought he threw that little act out there to tease his mother. Or put me on the spot. Or hell, bug the shit out of his father. But the way he says it now? It's like he's proud and wishful. Within this moment I choose for it to be real because a longing spikes inside me and warms my chest. I would be damn proud to belong to him. Even if he's already claimed me as his ol'lady and all of this is jumping from seed to fully grown.

Jag takes my hand in both of his, bringing it to his mouth to place a kiss on it while his eyes are locked with Calix's. Jag's eyes are filled with amusement, he's clearly taunting Calix and that somehow snags me. There's been enough stress tonight, I don't feel like adding another brand of aggravation.

I rip my hand away, wipe it off on my dress and place it on Calix's chest while I cuddle closer to him. Calix grasps my chin, tilts my head and places a gentle, swift kiss on my mouth.

"Jag is an asshole, Ten. But he's the right kind. He's one of the idiot friends I went to high school with back in the states," Calix tells me.

"You can shut up now before you start to spew shit about the time we were at that bar with the," Jag starts but Calix punches him in the shoulder.

"Yeah, shutting up would be good." Calix shakes his head. "Where is your lovely wife anyway?"

"Back home. Milli is sick. She was puking her four-year-old guts out, so we flipped a coin who would stay home and who would attend the party. But I think I've shown my face long enough. I was about to head out until I saw you. I had to come over and say hi."

"Be sure to say hi to Stella and Milli for me. We're heading out as well," Calix replies.

"Ah." Tag chuckles. "Overstayed your welcome,

or are you hightailing out of here?"

"Both I guess," Calix answers.

The two say their goodbyes and right after we make sure to acknowledge Calix's mother one more time before we slip out the front door and head back to the hotel.

CHAPTER ELEVEN

CALIX

Anger and irritation are still flowing through me. Though some already faded due to Tenley, but still…I need to punch something. Go to the gym or do anything to shake this feeling. Fuck. Why in the hell did I come here anyway? Especially with Ten by my fucking side. No one knows the entire truth. Well, Big Oaks knows because he pulled me out of the dark pit I was slipping into when I turned sixteen.

I might have tipped over if it wasn't for him. My mom left to spend three weeks alone with her sister for God knows why. Luckily my father turned a one eighty after that, but it didn't matter. I left and didn't look back, went into the Navy straight after and only kept in contact with my mother until I got out and maintained a brief meeting once every year since then. That's the only time I face my father. My mom and I do keep in contact through phone calls and texts.

I look toward the bed I just slipped out of. Ten drifted off to sleep right after I took her hard the second I closed the door. I shoved her against it, pulled up her dress, ripped away her thong, unleashed my hard cock and didn't stop pounding until I emptied myself inside her.

Like a madman heading for a goal. It wasn't just to blow off steam or to get off for that matter. I needed to possess her. She was right there with me tonight. For the first fucking time I didn't face him alone. I didn't fucking tell her anything but somehow she knew or figured out enough. She knew exactly what I needed and stepped up. And I fucking loved it. *I love her.*

Fuck. I love her. That realization hits. And when I glance over that angelic face, all carefree, and sated… there's no denying the fact that I do. Hence the reason I didn't even think to throw on a condom. Even if I fucked her bare before, I know now that I won't ever be wrapping up again. No need since I'm going to slide a ring on her finger as soon as I've bought one.

Ten stirs, her lashes flutter and her eyes meet mine. A sensual smile spreads her lips as she holds out her hand to me. "Come to bed, honey. I need you."

My feet move automatically. My mind doesn't even think. She calls, I fucking come. That's how shit like that works. Our fingers entwine and yet again some of the anger inside me fades. It's as if she keeps me grounded.

"You know," she mutters, sitting up and suddenly she doesn't look as if she was still sleeping a moment ago. "We did agree to have sex and have a discussion. We had the sex…just so you know we'll be doing that again in just a bit…but we haven't had the talk yet. I'm fine if you don't want to but you seem so tight, and it's because of that asshole, I know…but…you know. If you want, I'm right here."

"If it wasn't for your father, I don't think I would still be walking the Earth," I tell her in all honesty.

Sliding into the bed beside her, I actual revel in the fact that she doesn't say anything but only cuddles close.

"My whole family tree is old money with high class status. Meaning my father, grandfather, his father before him, and so on were hard bastards who had a mindset they drilled into their sons. They needed to be ruthless to handle any situation. No pussies but hard businessmen who don't back down. Inside as cold as stone and don't allow emotions to overtake you. That shit isn't taught in schools but it's taught behind closed doors, with a belt to the back. Something that's kept well buried...something the wives don't need to know because they soften up the sons." Staring straight ahead, I take comfort in stroking Ten's hair as I continue. "I wanted to tell my mother so many times. Yet I knew I couldn't. According to everything I've been taught by my father that would be a weakness. Women were to be kept out of men's business. *I had to be strong.* If I fucked up or wasn't acting accordingly, I was reprimanded. Meaning my father would whip me with his belt. And if I'd really pissed him off he'd use the buckle side of it. One night I couldn't take it anymore and screamed. I never fucking screamed because that also was considered a weakness. A man never cried or screamed, but the buckle sliced my back up a few days before already." Twisted, I fucking know, but a chuckle leaves my throat at the memory why I had to endure so much. "I wasn't an easy teenager. I acted up a lot. Fuck…I even challenged my father many times with my mother in the room, knowing he couldn't do anything until my mother left to visit a friend. And when she did I'd be long gone but that was only prolonging the inevitable. I'd get the whipping either way."

I feel wetness sliding down my bare chest and when I look down, I can see Ten's tearstained face.

"Aw, sweetness, don't spill tears for my fucked-up past. It's just that…the past," I tell her and even if this shit is rooted inside me, it's just that…a part of me I've learned to live with. "The hatred I have for that man lights up once a year when I have to endure a charity or two. But it's worth it because I get to see my mother. I damn well know his father did it to him, as his father before him. Maybe he doesn't think it's wrong to raise a child that way, I damn sure never asked. But as a kid I knew it wasn't normal and hell…I've pulled a lot of children out of homes for that exact reason during my law enforcement years."

"Your mother…does she?" Ten asks in a timid voice and that's a question that has been running through my mind for years too.

"I never asked. We never discussed anything. But she was raised within the same old money ring with the same principles and upbringing. When I left, I stayed with Big Oaks at the clubhouse, went into the military when I graduated high school, after that the clubhouse again while working hard to get the job I really wanted…I only talked to my mom about what was going on in my life, casual chitchat until about nine years ago when my mother took a bad fall. She spent a few weeks in the hospital but that made me realize I wanted to see more of her. I know the few days a year isn't much, but that's all I can manage since my dad won't ever leave her side."

"She loves him. And from what I saw she might be the only person he treats with respect." Ten yet again nails the hammer on the head.

"I know. But that's not how one should live their life. No fucking excuse," I growl.

Not angry at her but at everything that fucker did. Seems like he's still running my life after all these years.

"Sometimes you can't change a person's point of view. You have to step back and live your own life. You did that, Calix, and you still do. You stepped away. Not only that but you didn't turn out like your father, or his father before him."

"You don't know that." I hear myself say and suddenly realize the crucial fact that I might turn out like him at a later point in life when I've got a son myself. I fucked her bare. She might be pregnant right now. What if...

"Hey," Ten snaps, her hand cupping my face so our gaze connects. "Don't go there. I bet my own fucking life on it. You're a beautiful soul, Calix. You're an honorable man. From everything I've seen, you treat everyone with the same respect you receive. You've come so damn far and even have risen above the person who you should respect but can't because of the lack he showed you. And you're right you know...I'm glad you pushed me to get away for a few days. To come here and meet your parents and not tell me all of this up front. Or the fact that you jumped to claiming me as your ol'lady. You're right about all of it...the getting to know each other, we needed this. But Calix…you're very wrong when you think you will turn out like your father. There's just no way that's even possible."

The kiss she gives me after her words hits me just as hard. So much emotion and meaning behind all of it. I've bared a huge chunk of my life to her and she gracefully took it, embraced all of it. *All of me*.

Every single spark of tension that held my body hostage is draining away. I've got no need to punch a wall, or shit like that…all I need is the woman that's climbing on top of me. The feel of her naked body, skin on skin contact, her mouth devouring mine. In this moment we're two humans who let the world fall away around us. Because there's nothing we need more than each other.

My hands roam her back when she breaks our kiss and starts to slide down my body, leaving a trail of teasing sparks with her tongue. Her eyes are on mine, lighting up with mischief and fuck…a load of lust is burning so bright, I might blow my load before she can take me into her mouth. Because that's where she's heading.

Gentle fingers cup my heavy sack as she rolls it in her hand. Fucking hell, I seriously don't think I'm going to last long because when her little pink tongue starts to dart around the head of my cock…it's like sparks of electricity bouncing with pleasure are building inside me.

"Take me deep, Tenley," I say, my voice dark and raw with lust. "I want to hit the back of your throat and feel you swallow around me. Now. I need it."

She fists my cock harder, short strokes while she slightly twists, taking just the head as she starts to suck. Her cheeks hollowing and her eyes pinned on me.

The brat is going against my orders but fuck… "So good," I groan. "Keep it. Fuck. Yes. Harder." Her tongue teases the sensitive part underneath the head and I'm a goner. "Ten…fuuuuuuuck," I grunt and rise my hips off the bed. My hands keeping her head in place as I empty myself inside her mouth.

My cock falls from between her lips and she lazily licks it one more time from balls to tip before crawling back up my body. I pull her close and hold her tight while I still struggle to catch my breath.

"I'm going to eat your pussy in a minute or two

when I've got some energy back into my system. I need to return the favor because, damn…that was some serious blow job perfection. If I haven't asked for your hand yet…I would now," I tell her in all sincerity.

"My hand, huh? I thought you got all your energy drained out of you, but you're already asking for a hand job right after a blow job. Nice, Calix." She chuckles.

I smack her ass hard, making her yelp. "You know what I mean, woman."

She snuggles closer. "I know," she says before a breath whooshes out with some words that are barely a whisper, but I hear them damn fucking fine. "I just wanted my ass smacked."

Flashing up, she falls onto the bed where I flip her over on all fours, smacking that fine ass twice before I grip her hip with one hand while the other is holding her around the neck, pinning her to the bed.

"I won't tolerate being manipulated, Ten. So instead of getting spanked, you're getting a different punishment." Fuck. There might not be a difference because every smack that lights up her skin makes her pussy drip even more.

"I'm going to take what belongs to me and you,

sweetheart. You're not allowed to come. But I do have a present. I've bought it special for you. And no, it's not a ring but I'll be sure to buy one very soon." Standing up, I reach for the bag where I put in a few anal plugs and lube.

I damn well knew she'd be the feisty brat I craved beforehand. This being one of the most pleasurable ways for the both of us to handle things. Things like this…for me to show who's in charge, for her to see how far she can push me. Well, she's about to find out.

She sees what I have in my hands, her eyes going wide. "What's…what are you going to do with that?"

"That, sweetness, is the tiniest anal plug. Something we need to get you ready for my cock to fill up that tight ass of yours. I can't bury myself inside you yet, but I will own you in every place so we're going to prepare you for that. And this little plug is the first step. Don't worry…it's the size of my finger, I could use that but then I won't get to stare at your ass being filled up with a sparkly jewel staring up at me instead of that tight ring of yours. Look." I show her the silver colored plug that's got a red jewel on the back. "Fucking magnificent. That's going to look gorgeous decorating your ass when my cock is sliding in and out of your pussy. But it doesn't compare to what it will feel like, sweetness. Being filled up in two places, my cock rubbing against the plug through that tight membrane. Yeah."

I grab my cock that's already hard as fuck from the vision I just described. But my lust spikes when I hear her moan. Fucking hell, her fingers are already at work rubbing her clit.

"Are you getting yourself off with just me talking about what I'm going to do? What did I just tell you? You're not allowed to come, and for damn sure not allowed to pleasure the pussy that belongs to me, clear?" My voice is hard and my gaze is fixed on the hand that's slowly sliding away from her clit.

"Better," I croak as I place a knee on the bed.

Squirting an amount of lube over her tight ring, I start to rub my thumb over it. She tightens and it makes me smack her ass.

"Relax," I tell her and grab hold of my cock, sliding it back and forth along her slit before I slide home.

Slowly thrusting inside her, I reach for the plug and start to tease her ass with it. She's so caught up in the feeling of my cock filling her up that the extra element leaves her to push back on the plug, searching for more. My cock fills her and slides out, the plug sliding in. Repeating this several times before ultimately, I leave the plug in, letting the jewel sparkle at me. Fuck, that's magnificent.

I grab her hips and start to take her with force. Ten moans loudly, her hands are fisting the sheets as she begs me to go harder. Sweat is running down my back, my balls are slapping against her clit as they curve around with force. The raw grunts that leave my body are foreign to me. I've never given myself so hard and raw to anyone. She draws it out. All of it, letting me become the man that holds nothing back.

I relish in the fact that she begs me to let her come. Telling me with grunts and rapid breaths that she can't take it anymore, she needs it, *needs me*.

"Now," I roar, taking the plug to slide it out and back in one more time before I throw it on the bed to regain my grip on her hips. Her pussy obliges and strangles my cock with so much force it takes my last spark of energy to drag out and back in before I feel myself explode inside of her.

Sex this raw and intense is off the charts. Conversations with her are deep and meaningful. Her personality is warm and captivating. She's gorgeous as fuck and she's all mine. With those last thoughts, I wrap my arm around her waist and roll us to the side. Finally, my mind and body feel at peace and I owe it all to her.

CHAPTER TWELVE

TENLEY

Getting your ass spanked and filled up with a sparkly plug isn't something one should do when you have a long ass flight ahead of you. Dammit. I shift in my seat for the thousandth time as Calix smirks down on me.

I have the insane urge to lash out but that would only get me more smacks on my ass. Believe me, there's nothing more a turn on than that man smacking my ass but right now? I want to get home and sleep. It's been hours since we packed up, left the hotel, and took the long flight home. Let's not forget the bike ride back to my father's house we just took.

Calix guides me to the house, the door swings open and my father rushes out to pull me into a hug. "Damn, I missed your crazy ass," he mutters into my neck.

"Pretty sure that's my line." I giggle and hug him tight.

We all stroll inside and when I get into the living room, I see Dams, Hugo, and C.Rash occupying the couch and several chairs.

"Hey, man." Calix pats Dams on the shoulder. "You heading out later today?"

"In a few hours, we need to catch up on a few things first," Dams says in a low voice.

Which is weird because though Calix switched chapters, I'm still a VP, not to mention his ol'lady. "What's going on?" I question, hoping to get a straight answer but instead Dams shrugs.

"Nothin' just something private I wanted his opinion on." Dams, the fucker, lies his ugly ass off.

"Suuuuure." I roll my eyes and grab my bag. "I'm gonna put this away and freshen up, I'll be downstairs in a bit. Oh, Prez, does our car wash still have clients or did the guys steal all my girls and kept them busy in a whole different way?"

"Steal your girls?" Calix questions.

"I brought my car up and had it washed three fuck-ing times a day," C.Rash groans. "Yo, VP, think Zack will let me transfer here too?"

"What the hell, man?" Calix snaps.

"Your ol'lady earned that VP patch for a reason. She deserved that title and she's given the club a steady money flow since. It's not because she's my daughter that she got that patch. Fuck no. She earned it fair and square. And as you can hear, she's back one damn sec-ond and already she's got her mind back on business to check if everything went well. She's a brilliant busi-ness woman," My Prez says.

Yeah, My Prez. Because that man has two sides for me and sometimes they do mix. But when we're at the club or discussing club business, it's my Prez. When it's personal or around the house, he's my father. In the beginning he had the two mixed, never letting me do anything too risky. Luckily he toned it down when he saw I could handle myself perfectly. Well except for what happened with Dane. But even then, he stepped up and had me bring in Calix. And he was right about that too.

"That bikini car wash was the most brilliant idea ever, man," Hugo beams. "She's got a menu to pick what gal is gonna wash your car when you're inside it. Hooooooooottttttt."

When Calix turns to me his look shows me he's furious. Why the hell would he be angry?

"Tell me right the fuck now that you're not on that menu," he hisses through his teeth.

I bite my bottom lip, grab my bag and dash out of the room, throwing over my shoulder, "Be right back, gonna go freshen up."

Uh huh, then I won't tell him. Way better than the other option because my ass is still sore and I'm not taking any punishments for things that happened before we got together. I make a mental note to reprint the menus and pull my name off them.

I'm about to close the door of my bedroom when it's caught by Calix's huge frame. "Oh, no you're not. Now answer the damn question."

"I'll reprint the menu, okay?" There. Safe enough.

"I'll reprint...motherfucker," he growls.

"How many times have you," He doesn't finish his sentence but groans and tugs his short hair.

I step up to him and slide my arms around his waist. "I'm mostly busy with running the car wash and the girls get to decide what to wear. They don't like my outfit too much because the others pick different sets and get more tips that way. I'm more cut out for running the business anyway."

"I want to know and deep down I damn well don't. Let's just quit talking about this. And no damn way my ol'lady will be on a menu." His voice sounds pained and somehow this attitude does something for me.

Though I was always one who wore shorts and a t-shirt or a tank top, other girls wear tight and tiny bikinis earning way more tips and more requests. The first request I got was from Dane. Surprise, surprise. Well, his disappointment was clear when I showed up in shorts and a thick t-shirt that didn't even show my sports bra I had underneath. The thought still makes me chuckle.

"What's the thing Dams wants to discuss without me being there?" I question.

Calix gives me a quick kiss, pulls back and shrugs his shoulders. "I don't know. I'll hear what he has to say soon enough."

"Are we going to have secrets between us? And I don't mean I have to know every single detail, but I do like to be in the know and not have things go around my back because that kind of shit would really piss me off."

"Understood, VP." Calix chuckles.

And that's the second time he's called me VP. That fast he knows the difference like I have with my father...the line between personal and business.

"Hmmm," I croon. "I like the sound of that. Makes me wonder how good you're willing to follow orders."

"There's a line, Tenley. You and me in the bedroom or where ever we are going to fuck, that's going to put me in charge at all times. In the clubhouse or among brothers if the situation calls for it, you're the VP. Other than that, you're my ol'lady. Clear?"

"Good to know you've got your dildos in a row." I laugh and jump out of his grasp.

"I'll show you all the dildos in a row when I shove them inside you one at a time," he growls, making me dash over the bed to have something in between us.

"I was only joking!" I squeak. "About everything. You know I was."

"I never joke about those things, sweetness. Surely not the nice set of plugs I bought just for you."

"You are supposed to buy a girl a ring with a jewel…not sparkly plugs instead of a ring! The sparkly thing needs to be on my finger not in my ass," I joke, yet again.

But Calix pulls up the sleeves of his Henley, placing those gloriously inked up forearms and hands on show. Putting one hand on his bicep, the other grasping his chin, as if he's thinking things through. "Is that so?"

We're interrupted when Dams knocks on my bedroom door, making Calix turn around. "Hey. Sorry to interrupt, but I really need ten minutes of your time, man."

Calix throws me a glance and says, "I'll be right back."

After I give him a nod, he leaves the bedroom. This gives me the time to freshen up because I feel all kinds of icky after the long flight.

When I'm walking back into the living room, my hair still wet from the long shower I took, I'm surprised to find only Hugo and C.Rash sitting across from each other.

"Hey," I quip, a tiny fragment annoyed by the fact that Calix, Dams, and my father aren't there. Even more due to the fact that I can see them standing in the back yard. All the way back all huddled close.

"Hey, VP. Do you have any idea what those guys are discussing?" Hugo asks me, a grin sliding in place. "I bet your ol'man doesn't hold anything back, huh?"

Oh, for the love of God. We get that already? Some bikers are like little gossip grannies. No way am I going there. Not only because I'm the damn VP, but mostly I don't spill anything that goes on between my ol'man and me. Dude talk. All I've ever been around for the last few years are bikers talking dirty.

Best to turn things around in their style. "My ol'man holds nothing back, Hugo." I smirk. "Especially when he's taking me hard. And he does this thing where he adds a,"

"Don't want to know." C.Rash flashes up from the couch and covers his ears. "Don't fucking say it. I've seen a video and what that man is capable off. Not just no, fuck to the hell and back, no. That man of yours has the kind of skills that scares the piss out of me."

Calix's laughter fills the room. I didn't even notice they walked in. "What were you guys talking about to get C.Rash flipping his shit?"

"I could ask you the same thing, brother. Need some help?" Hugo steps closer to Calix. "You know I'm always here for you."

"I know, man." Calix slaps Hugo on the back. "I can always count on you. But this was something I needed to wrap up for Zack. Now everything is dealt with for the other chapter and I'm all Ohio chapter now, brother."

"Fuck, yeah," Hugo bellows and grabs Calix by the front of his jacket. "No more suits, fucker."

Calix snorts. "I'll be wearing my cut from now on but I'm not ditching the suits any time soon. My ol'lady gets soaking wet when I'm wearing one." He throws me a wink, making me swoon.

"No! I said no to sharing sexcapades from you guys." C. Rash covers his ears again.

I make a mental note to ask why C.Rash acts this way and yet I don't know if I'm ready to hear it… would it be freaky? Freaky enough to spook that biker. Yet I know Calix would never hurt me, well…as long as pleasure is involved.

"Okay, you guys. It's been a long day and I've got a few hours of road to burn. Calix," Dams gives Calix a man-hug, "come by soon, fucker."

"Will do, brother," Calix promises.

"Tenley, congratulations are in order," Dams says and gives me a quick hug before stepping back. "And I'll see you very soon too."

"Thank you. Say hi to your ol'lady and to Blue for me," I beam.

His words mean a lot but the look on his face tells me he's sincere and the private discussion he wanted with Calix suddenly made sense. I mean, this is really it...Calix left his chapter and is now a part of the Ohio chapter.

"Will do. Enjoy your evening, folks. I'm hitting the road." Calix walks him out while my father turns to me.

"Did you guys have anything to eat before you came here? Did you want me to grab something from the freezer or order something?" he questions.

"We grabbed something on the way over. If you don't mind I'll take my ol'lady and cut the evening short. I didn't sleep on the plane and I'm tired as fuck," Calix says, walking back into the room.

"That sounds better than food," I admit. "I'm tired and that shower did nothing to wake me up."

"That's because you always take hot ones. I've warned you before about that, it's not good for your body," my father says.

I roll my eyes. "Yeah, Dad. I know. But I'm not into cold showers."

I shiver at the thought. He always complains when he catches me walking out of the shower in my robe, calves flaming red. I can't help it…I love hot showers.

"Catch you guys tomorrow," Calix says and guides me up the stairs.

Once there, he strips and heads for the bathroom. I let him take his time to shower while I take off my clothes and slide into bed. I grab one of my favorite paperbacks from the table beside the bed. I love to reread a few pages if I can't seem to fall asleep quick enough. This keeps me entertained until Calix strolls back naked into the bedroom. Dammit, this man is tempting.

"Yeah, forget about it. Not now, I wasn't kidding, Tenley. I'm dead tired. If it's not from the fight, it's from the shit that's coming up." Calix sighs and shakes his head.

I put away the book and click off the lamp on the bedside table, plunging the room into darkness.

Calix pulls me to him. "Besides, with your father inside the house, I wouldn't want to stuff panties into your mouth to mute the sound. I happen to like hearing you scream when you orgasm beautifully."

I groan. "Shut up. Because we might need to do that anyway since I won't stop having sex with you. It's either that or only fuck when he's not home or if we're in my room back at the clubhouse."

"That's our room at the clubhouse, and when this shit is over, we'll buy a place of our own," Calix vows.

"Hmmmm," I hum. "That sounds perfect." I'm drifting off being this comfortable and wrapped in his arms.

"You're the one who's perfect." Calix nuzzles my neck. "Just remember, Tenley...whatever happens, trust only me. I've got you, okay? Always."

"Always," I murmur, half asleep already.

CHAPTER THIRTEEN

CALIX

Fuck. My chest tightens at what's about to come. It's inevitable and I damn well wish there was another way but all options have slipped through our fingers.

"Ten, wake up." Nothing. She's still sleeping so I make my next words snap out. "VP, wake the fuck up."

She jolts awake, swinging her head from left to right until her eyes land on mine. "What? What is it?"

I soften my voice and let sadness hit me. "It's your father, sweetness."

One should think in all my long years with law enforcement, bringing the news about a dead family member should be rehearsed plenty, right?

Know exactly what to say and shit. Yeah, fuck that. Every time it's even worse.

"He's gone."

"Gone?" She jumps off the bed and throws on her jeans along with a sweater. Pulling on her boots she questions, "Where did he go?"

Stalking over, I pull her close and tell her. "He's gone, sweetness. He died in his sleep last night. C.Rash found him this morning. We called the doc and he just confirmed."

"No," she whispers before a louder version rips from her throat and she starts to struggle.

"Calm down, Ten. The doc is still in there, we need to give him a minute."

"You're bullshitting me, he was fine yesterday!" she seethes.

"I know, that's why the doc is double checking everything. We'll go to him in a minute or two, okay?"

She doesn't listen but rips free and runs down the hall. Following her, I watch as she pushes Hugo out of the doorway. C.Rash is standing near the bed and catches Tenley just in time before she launches herself at her father.

"So sorry, darlin' he was a good man. Come on, you don't need to see this." C.Rash comforts her, his gaze meeting mine. "Calix, come and guide your woman out while we handle this for her. Hugo, can you call the brothers? Let them know?"

Tenley swallows and steps back from C.Rash, her gaze pinned on her father while tears slide down her cheeks. "Hugo. Listen to C.Rash. Inform everyone and get them all to the clubhouse. We'll be there later. Go, I will…Calix and I will handle it."

"Sure thing, VP." Hugo nods and looks at me. "Or does she become the Prez, now that her father is gone."

"What the fuck, dude?" I growl, smacking him on the back of his head. "Listen to your VP and get that shit done."

"Sorry. Yeah. Will do. I'll head over to the club-house, see you there." Hugo rushes off. I carefully follow him down the stairs and make sure the door is locked behind him.

I take the stairs two at a time and rush back into the bedroom. "Yeah?" I ask C.Rash, making sure he sees I'm glancing around the room, silently asking the question he will understand.

"We're clear, brother. No bugs. I scanned twice. The only ones watching us are…well, us." He chuckles.

"Thank fuck," I mutter and stalk over to Ten, cup her face and make her look at me.

Dammit those damn tears along with the sorrow and grief are slicing straight through my heart. This couldn't be helped and yet it feels so damn wrong within this moment.

"Big Oaks," I snap. "All clear, Prez."

Ten's eyes go wide before I let her go so she can turn her head toward her father who jolts up from the bed. "Cerise, come here. I'm so sorry, sweetheart. We had to, there was no other way."

"What's going on?" Ten takes a step back, confused as fuck, and why shouldn't she be?

"Dams put up cameras a few days ago when your father contacted Zack. Big Oaks knew something was coming and he got help before this shit got real, because what just happened wasn't something we set up…well, we did…but if it wasn't for the cameras, your father would have taken his medicine and would have died in his sleep because of it. Hugo can't be trusted.

210

He switched your father's meds, Ten."

"Sonofabitch," Ten growls and tries to leave the room.

I can barely wrap my arm around her waist to get her back inside. "Hold on a sec. We've planned this part. We're betting on the fact that Hugo is going straight to Dane. Think, Ten. They think your dad, the Prez, is dead. That means we're going to walk straight into a trap once we head over to the clubhouse."

I can tell by the way her upper lip rises in anger that all of this has settled in. "What's the next step?" she snaps but jabs a finger into my pecs. "And don't think I will forget about the fact that you cut me off, deliberately shutting me out, making me think my father is dead. Such a dick move, mister."

"That was my call," Big Oaks states. "We needed it to be as real as possible, Cerise. Hugo has known Calix for a long damn time, and you too for over seven years…he would have known if you faked shock and grief, sweetheart. We couldn't risk it."

"Fine," she snaps once more. "Just tell me what the next move is."

Yeah. I'm damn sure that if we're going to pull

through this that I'm still going to wish I was dead because I don't think she's ever going to forgive me.

"Now all of us are going to get killed." C.Rash chuckles and shoots her a wink.

"That's the plan," I quip.

Big Oaks starts to talk, the doc is still in the room because that's one brother that we do trust. We've brought him in from the Chicago chapter. It's a damn pain we need to drag brothers from different parts to flush out the bad seed in the Ohio chapter but there just isn't any other way.

"Are you sure about this?" Ten asks her father for a second time when we're about to leave the house.

"Yes, VP," he tells her with a stern voice.

She nods and gives him one last hug. "I love you."

"Love you too, baby. Now let your man handle this. Let him have your back," Big Oaks whispers but his eyes are on me and I know he's saying it loud enough for me to hear so it goes for me too.

I give the man a nod to let him know I understand. I'll do anything for her, no questions asked. And if there was a way, I would keep her out of this, but I can't. We've discovered that not only Big Oaks, but

Ten too, has a target on her head. They want her dead and out of their way. Where Dane wanted her as his ol'lady…she's considered a whore now, one who needs to be disposed of.

Oh, yeah. We've bugged every room in the clubhouse around the same time we put cameras into Big Oaks' house. When he called Zack and relayed some of his suspicions they didn't take it lightly. I mean, Big Oaks' bike was tampered with and he discovered his meds were off too. He might be old but when you take a specific kind of meds on a daily basis for years you know when there's even a slight change in the prescription. He caught it this time but that was a risk he couldn't take lightly.

The decision to keep Tenley out of all of this was because she was too wrapped up in it. Besides it being a request from Big Oaks to keep his daughter safe, she was also at risk due to her fierce temper toward Dane. We wanted to gather enough evidence to let him tie a noose around his neck himself. And he did. We got it all on tape too. That's why we've got two other chapters in on it to make sure the verdict will prevail.

So now we're heading to the clubhouse where we

know for sure at least six brothers have been plotting the murder of their Prez and VP. Like hell I'm going to let them point one damn finger my ol'lady's way. I'm going to rip their fucking brains out, this ends today.

I tug at my cut which is feeling way too fucking tight when Ten comes up from behind me and slaps my hand away. "Stop fidgeting. Let's go."

"Remember," I whisper. "Sadness, Ten. Keep up appearances or bite their head off for that matter. Your dad just died and they expect to see a woman that's torn up and emotional."

She full-on glares at me, making me smirk. "Keep that up and I'll grab that bigger plug with the green jewel tonight."

"Looking forward to it." Her damn eyes twinkle.

"That's a promise then," I growl and connect our mouths for a scorching, lightning fast kiss. Remembering the taste of her before we risk our damn lives.

C.Rash walks up front. I scan the surroundings one more time, knowing this can turn bad real fast. No matter how well we talked this through.

I feel Ten's hand grabbing mine. She gives a little

squeeze. "We got this, Calix. All of us. This has to be done, no matter the consequences."

My fingers wrap around her throat. "Don't fucking die on me," I growl.

"Yeah, that would suck. So right back at you," she growls back.

"Showtime, fuckers," C.Rash mutters.

The clubhouse is crowded. Every member is present. Even Dane who's standing around Ryke, Steel, and Beck. Hugo leans in to say something to Dane who nods and slides his eyes to me.

"Church," Dane bellows. "Now."

He steps up to Ten, his face a fake mask of sympathy. "I'm so sorry, Cerise."

"Don't call me that," she snaps. "Don't even talk to me. And what reason do you have to call church for? You're not even allowed in here, did you forget? Because I sure as fuck didn't. How dare you be in here and act like you didn't betray another brother. And on the day my father, our Prez, dies? Get out, Dane. Get out and don't come back."

"Why? Because you think you're the President now? Did you really think any of us would allow a cunt to take the gavel? You've been tolerated long enough but that ends now." Dane sneers before he steps back and throws his hand in the air. "Brothers. I would have done it first in church to get everyone up to speed but I might as well get it all in the open right now."

His eyes find mine and the glow in his eyes make the hairs on the back of my neck stand on end.

"I have proof that this fucker right here swapped Big Oaks meds. He's killed our Prez, brothers. He's the one who betrayed our trust."

The clubhouse goes dead silent before all eyes are on me.

Dane takes the advantage and starts to ramble some more. "He's been planning this all along. He wants the gavel, the one he turned down all those years ago. Calix thinks he can walk back in here with the support of another chapter and take over this club. Remember when my father, and fuck…some of you too, voted for him to be VP after my father had the accident? He was for a few months, knowing he would be in Big Oaks' chair one day but then he got that job offer, to become a detective, and dropped all of us. Thinking he was better than all of us. Now he got his ass fired because they caught him doing something…he got an honorable discharge. What did you think, asshole? Time to pick shit back up? Fool some more people? Fool brothers? You're the fool if you think you can walk back in, asshole."

The self-absorbed gloat he gives me slides onto the face of his supporters who are standing behind him. There are six already and even though Big Oaks talked to most of the loyal brothers a few days ago…doubt is now thrown in the mix and I hope to fuck this is going to end well. I glance at Ten's face and my chest squeezes. It does look like I've got a lot more to lose.

CHAPTER FOURTEEN

TENLEY

No. Dane is talking bullshit. Calix quit his job as a detective. He doesn't want to be a Prez. He told me this. My father is still alive…he told me Hugo switched the meds…he told me. Fuck. *I never saw proof.* I don't have the nerve to take a glance at Calix. My gut tells me Dane is full of bullshit. But there's a little spike of doubt that makes me wonder. And that almost kills me.

I want to scream and punch Dane in the face, grab Calix so he can tell me about the lies and truth…but I can't. Now I get the loaded looks my brothers are giving me. They are waiting for me to freak out. To show them I've got a cunt, and those who have them don't have the ability to have high positions in a man's world. Fuck that. Anger fills my veins for a whole lot of reasons. So damn much that there's an eerie calm settling inside me.

"Church," I say in a cold and clear voice and stalk off.

I hear footsteps following me but there's not one word being spoken. When I sit down in my father's chair, I throw a look toward Dane who's shooting me a deadly glare.

"Do you have a problem with me taking lead, Dane? Because I know for damn sure I've got the VP patch on my tit, not you. Sit your ass down and show us the evidence to back up the words you just spilled." I don't even recognize my cold voice when I glance around the table that's now filled with brothers who've always had my father's back.

"VP," Ryke says from my right. "You're in mourning, we can do this later."

"We're here now. We're going to handle it now," I snap back at the man who voted for Dane, so for me, he's on Dane's side.

Dane takes out a piece of paper and lays it down in

front of me. "That's the name of a cop who just dragged a guy out of a river who works at a pharmacy. Calix got the meds from this guy. You can validate everything, it's clear as day what Calix's intentions have been from the start."

I take the piece of paper and stare at the letters. Throwing them back on the table, I simply state, "I have it on good authority that Hugo was the one who switched the meds."

"That shows it, doesn't it?" Dane bellows with his arms wide. "Those fuckers were best buddies before Calix left." He throws Hugo a look. "Did he promise you VP status, that it?"

Hugo's face hardens in anger. "You made me fucking do it with that promise, asshole. You told me we would turn this club around and take the weapon deal Bartini offered along with the hundred grand bonus for becoming his new pipeline."

Everyone starts to talk at the same time. I smack my hand on the table like I've seen my father do lots of times. "Shut it. One thing at a fucking time," I bellow, regaining silence yet again.

"Dane, you were already demoted but hearing

some new elements and the damn reason why you wanted to be Prez yourself, and with that are responsible for the intention of killing my father, our Prez. You are getting my vote, the one where you're going to meet your maker," I state matter-of-factly.

"I second this," Hugo states.

All around the table voices of agreement ring out. Dane realizes his time is up. Reaching for his gun, he pulls it out in a flash and has it aimed at my head within the next instant.

I should be scared. I should know my time could be up with my next breath. I should be a lot of things and yet there's nothing I've got to lose within this moment. A few hours ago, I thought my father had died. He's still very much alive and yet I know he won't be with me for much longer due to his illness.

The things Dane threw out, causing me to have doubt of Calix's intentions slashed a hurt bigger than knowing we're going to have to face Bartini. A major player in the gun business who's been trying to set foot in our city for a while now. If Dane made a promise, this club is doomed to face a war with this man and his small army. You might as well say death and despair will fill our future anyway.

"Go ahead, Dane. Pull the damn trigger. It will be your last move anyway. We both know your ass will never sit on this chair and I can honestly tell you that this is the last time mine will warm it too. Since my father is very much alive." The shock of my words registers on Dane's face as words of disbelief flow through the words from other brothers.

A gunshot rings out. Dane's body falls to the floor at the same moment Ryke states, "That fucker has annoyed me for the last damn time."

"Put the gun down, Ryke," Calix states in a cold voice, his gun aimed at Ryke.

Ryke swings his head toward Calix. "You first, asshole. I might have played by Big Oaks' rules for the last few weeks, but after hearing all of this shit, I need to know what your intentions are and where your loyalty lies. According to Big Oaks, he told all of us he would like you to be our Prez when his time came. That true? Even when this fucker," he kicks Dane's body, "might have brought a new load of trouble on our doorstep. You still want to sit in that chair? I know you have the funding to back up a war if it gets to that, but will you?"

"Those are a lot of questions, Ryke," Calix states, putting his gun away as he sits down.

Everyone is still silent and so am I. To be honest, I have no damn clue what to do and say. We had Zack and many of the brothers of the other chapter surrounding the clubhouse because we were expecting…I don't know…hell, me, Calix, and C.Rash are wearing bulletproof vests. That says enough, right?

So, no. I didn't know what to expect, neither one of us thought that within a club with something as big as this would be settled in church with a single bullet. It's too damn easy and yet what they just said about Bartini will be the biggest thing this club has ever faced.

Well, from what I've heard that is because I was only allowed full information a few months ago when I became VP. A full member instead of the daughter who worked the books and knew everything there was to know about the club financially.

Though I know very well that what the club needs right now isn't a woman in this position. "Everyone put their guns away and sit your asses down. We're going to get the Prez in here. C.Rash, call Zack and let my dad know to get his old ass in here. But I would like to have a word with my father first, so I need for all of you to get out of here, grab a beer and come back when the dead body has been brought outside and my father and I are done."

Most nod and start to slip out of the room. C.Rash turns his attention to me as he puts away his phone. "He's on his way."

It takes a moment before church is empty. Ryke and C.Rash grab Dane's body and drag him out. Calix goes to the door and bellows to C.Rash. "Make sure Hugo doesn't leave and all of you, keep an eye on the other Dane groupies because we're not done with you fuckers yet. Oh, and C.Rash...don't dispose of Dane just yet. We need him to get a message across to Bartini. Just put him in one of the barrels out back."

Calix closes the door and turns to me. "What are you going to do?"

Anger is visibly rolling off him. Hands clenching, eyes narrowing. Yet he has no reason to. I let Dane screw with my head only a flash of a moment. Dane knew how to word his statement well enough to try and make dents into some of Calix intentions.

Dane failed because all he ever did was tell lies while Calix has done nothing but show what he's worth. Hence the reason for what I'm about to do.

"Don't worry. I don't believe a word Dane said about you." I shrug out of my cut and shirt, ripping off the bulletproof vest before putting my shirt back on. I leave my cut on the table.

"I'm not talking about that shit. I damn well know you can see through lies, even if some sound logical and cause doubt. But you've gotten to know me so I hope to fuck you're as brilliant as I think you are and know bullshit from truth when you hear it," Calix growls. "I'm talking about you doing that." He points at my cut that's lying on the table.

"It's club business, Calix," I state at the same moment my father opens the door. "Go handle the stuff you had in mind, what you just told C.Rash."

"Ten," he hisses through his teeth. "Listen to me."

"You're dismissed, *brother*," I tell him, clearly letting him know it's not personal, it's business…something I need to do for the both of us.

"Go, Calix," my father states, holding the door open.

There's a vein on Calix's temple that's about to explode. I know he's angry at me, and hell…he might be furious when I walk out of here in a few minutes, but this has to be done.

Calix stomps out of church, leaving my father to close the door behind him. I take a seat and wait for my Prez to sit down.

"Prez," I address my father for the last time this way, my throat clogging up. "I need for you to let them take a vote."

"You sure, VP? Because I wanted to step back. I'm getting sicker and while I still got all my ducks in a row, I would rather see him filling my chair. Almost every brother in here knows him or has heard of him. They were all ready to vote him in. Nine brothers have been waiting for this moment for over eleven years. They have spent years with that man knowing how he is. There's no better person who can take my place. I thought you wanted to be VP, Cerise? Why turn in the patch? Why now while you can support your ol'man?"

"Because I'd rather be his ol'lady. He needs one of his brothers to be his VP. Hell, C.Rash would be the right choice since they've worked together for years with the other chapter, it would be good to have a fresh set to build things up again. You know how most will be, all thinking they want a shot but no one knowing how to handle shit. Didn't it show from the day I became VP? That says it all, right? This club needs strong shoulders to hold it together and rebuild." I grab my knife I strapped to my belt earlier today and work on getting the VP patch off.

When I'm done, I throw the patch on the table in front of me. "Make sure the brothers vote for the future of this club." I grab my cut and walk out the door.

CALIX

She's going to step back, I just fucking know it.

"Keep your head at the task at hand, brother. I got this shit all over me already. Fuck," C.Rash grunts as his fingers slip on Dane's skin again.

"Shut up and grab tight, I'm almost done," I tell him as I carve the last letter into Dane's stomach.

I wrote a few words for Bartini for when we drop Dane's body on his doorstep. The Ohio chapter of Areion Fury MC will never have anything to do with a weapon dealer. If Bartini is smart, he will back away. He might be a huge player, but I've got ties with a lot of law enforcement tasks and not to mention a lot of

Areion Fury MC chapters who will back us up. I will make sure this blows over, this club has been through enough.

"Make sure Feargal drops this fucker where Bartini's men will find him," I tell C.Rash and head back into the clubhouse.

I make a pit stop at the bathroom in the back to clean off the blood and take a piss. Strolling into the room that's filled with bikers, I get a lot of backslaps and words of praise. I'm sure the gossip factory is running in full force.

Zack grabs me by the shoulder. "You did well, brother."

"Yeah, yeah. But why did you have to blabber that shit around?" I grumble, knowing he told everyone in here it was my plan to bug rooms and draw Dane out the way we did.

Zack chuckles. "I'm sure you won't need it, but credit is due where it's due. No need to shy away from a job well handled."

"Hey…Ryke did the hard part with going undercover in his own damn club. Making believe he wanted Dane to be Prez. Big Oaks made the right decision to ask him to do so a few months ago, he saw it all coming. Besides…Ryke shot the fucker. Big Oaks is still here and a damn good Prez, it's all good, brother."

"Yeah? No regrets yet? Wanna come crawling back to our chapter?" Zack raises an eyebrow at me.

"Fuck no. My ol'lady is here, a part of this chapter. Well, maybe not because I think she's stepping back as VP." I sigh, remembering the look on her face when I walked out of church.

"You'll handle it." Zack nods, smacks my shoulder and says nothing more.

The door from church opens and Ten walks out. She's holding her cut in her hands but I can clearly see that she's removed the VP patch. She gives me a tight smile and steps toward me. Before she can reach me, Beck blocks her path. Fear hits my chest and yet I damn well know all brothers who backed up Dane were disarmed.

"This is all your fault, bitch. If you would have just took your place as Dane's ol'lady this whole club wouldn't be in the situation it is now." Beck has his hands around her throat in a flash.

I slowly move forward, ready to grab Beck, to

prevent him from snapping my woman's neck when I'm held back by Zack. Trying to shove him off me, he silently points at my woman.

Before I can jump between them, Ten snatches the knife she carries on her belt and plunges it in Beck's side. Lunging forward, Zack and I both drag Beck off, my fist hitting his face over and over until it's me who they're dragging off Beck.

"I think you killed him dead, brother." C.Rash chuckles and pats my chest.

Glancing around the clubhouse, I bellow, "Those who stood behind Dane, turn in your fucking cut. Those who won't stand behind your Prez...turn in your fucking cut. This ends today. Ohio chapter will be one solid front again. No. Fucking. Disloyalty. No. Fucking. Disrespect."

Hard grunts of agreement ring out while Steel, Hank, Bo, and Hugo are being dragged off. I'm torn between checking on my woman and handling business.

But she takes the choice out of my hands when she says, "Go, I'm fine."

I give her a nod before I follow my brothers out.

Like I just said…this ends today.

Fucking messy as shit and I don't think my killing rate has been as high on one day as it is today, but there wasn't any way around it. Thank fuck I already turned in my badge. Bringing these fuckers in for justice…for the attempted murder of their Prez, for one.

This shit isn't even going to be brought to the table. One of these fuckers who backed up Dane just tried to strangle my ol'lady. It's done. Their life is over, they've dug their grave and I'm going to make sure they'll be buried in it.

It takes over three hours to drag my ass back to the club. Feargal strolling in behind me along with Quillon and Keitel. Three other brothers already got back to the clubhouse before us because we had some more cleaning up to do. I might have gone a little overboard with releasing some steam before I killed the traitors.

"There he is!" Hunter bellows through the clubhouse, making me groan.

The fucker was jumping up and down when I threw Hugo through the air, snapping his neck before he hit the ground. I'm betting the idiot told every detail in full glory to all the brothers. Ignoring him, I scan the room for my woman. Seems I don't have to when a body hits me from the side. Legs circle around my waist as I grab Ten's ass and keep her close.

"Missed you," she tells me before her mouth crashes down over mine.

Catcalls should keep me from kissing her but instead I take this moment to get lost in our connection. I damn well deserved this moment. And it seems the both of us need it and yet know we have to keep things short.

Ten pulls back and places her forehead against mine. "We're sleeping in our room at the clubhouse tonight, deal?"

"Deal." I chuckle and let her slide down my body.

"Great timing, Calix." Zack reaches out, smacking me on the back. "I need to head back."

"I'll walk you guys out," I tell him.

Understanding the brothers have a long trip home, I make sure to thank every single one for coming over. It's damn good to know these guys will always have my back, even when I joined another chapter...these things will never change. Ten is standing beside me as we watch all the bikes leave the premises. Another fucking thing I hope will never change; *my woman standing strong beside me.*

CHAPTER SIXTEEN

Three weeks later

TENLEY

My eyes find the doors of church again, waiting for them to open. They've been in there for over an hour. How long do these things take? Ugh. Ever since I've stepped back from being a VP, I hoped this day would come. Or better yet…that the outcome will go as I hope it will.

The doors open and brothers start to flow out. Feargal shoots me a smile. Hunter nods furiously while Quillon gives me two thumbs up. This is it. Warmth along with joy blooms inside my chest but I don't allow myself to believe it. Not until I see it with my own eyes.

My father steps out and my eyes slide to his pecs. It's gone. The President patch is gone. Calix comes up behind him, my gaze hits the President patch. I squeal in delight and run toward him. Launching myself at him, he easily catches me and spins me around.

"You're the Prez!" I breathe.

"Yeah, sweetness. Unanimous vote. Same as C.Rash, as my VP," Calix tells me and another wave of joy hits me.

He told me this morning he wanted C.Rash as his VP. Something a lot of us saw coming. Every brother knew and today was only a formal thing but still, I was very nervous about all of it. When I look at Calix's face I can tell he's happy. Such a difference from weeks ago. When I met him he didn't look this relaxed or satisfied for that matter.

He took a lot of change to the table these last few weeks, all of it welcomed by the brothers, knowing they needed a change of leadership and mindset to get this chapter back to its old self. The way it was when my father was handling it with his full attention.

The past few months he missed a lot of time at the club because of his illness, leadership clearly missing at a time where vultures took their shot. I'm happy the club survived all of it. Things are finally falling into place. Not only for the club but also between me and Calix.

Meaning we are now officially house searching. Some place close to the club and my father. Though he doesn't have all the time left in this crazy world…he does intend to spend the rest of his time enjoying his life to the fullest. We've managed to move Gertie in with him. She's ten years younger than my father but it's clear there's something going on between them… more than her being his help around the house.

Though that's something I'll gladly ignore, but I'm happy he has someone when I'm not there to help out. It was him who pushed Calix and me to find our own house. He practically threatened Calix to suggest Fear-gal to be the Prez if we didn't move out soon. He was joking of course, but he made his point.

"Let's celebrate!" Quillon bellows through the clubhouse and turns the music on loud.

Calix chuckles, nuzzling my neck. "You want a beer, sweetness?"

"You trying to get me drunk, Prez?" I quip.

"Fuck no." Calix squeezes my ass. "I'm just giving you the option of drinking one beer before we head for our room. You've been taking a bigger plug every other night…you're ready to take my cock. Now that would be the perfect way to celebrate."

I can barely keep the moan inside with just the thought of him filling me up. We've been trying a lot of things lately and I must say…sex with this man is never boring. And I'm sure that after twenty years, this man will still manage to surprise me in bed.

"Yo, Prez. Come on, man. Bring your ol'lady, we need to drink!" C.Rash slaps Calix on the back.

We both follow him to the bar where a lot of brothers are already nursing their beer. Within this moment, we take the joy of the brotherhood. We still haven't heard anything from Bartini. And we damn well know he got Dane delivered to him with Calix's message. But everything has been silent.

Calix said we will handle anything that comes our way. He's got enough eyes and ears on the street to know ahead of time if something is coming. In this I believe and trust him, as do we all.

"You want that beer, sweetness?" Calix asks.

I shake my head. "No damn way. I intend to enjoy every second of tonight, and every day after. Clear head and all." I shoot him a wink. "Because life with you has already gotten me drunk on love."

C.Rash fake gags. "That was horrible. Please don't do that again."

Laughter rips from Calix's throat. "Shut it, idiot. That's my ol'lady right there. The woman who loves me just as much as I love her."

"No, no…" I tell him. "I'm positive I love you more."

C.Rash slaps his hands over his ears. "What the fuck you two? Cut with the mushy love statements. Aw, fuck, don't suck on each other's face in front of me…Yeah, I'm out of here. Yo, Quillon. Hand me that bottle of whiskey. I'm going to get myself drunk enough to pop some brain cells, hoping they are the ones where this fucked up mushy shit are stored so it doesn't come back to haunt me."

I'm already blocking C.Rash's voice out, surrendering to the way Calix claims my mouth exactly the way he claimed my heart. Taking, dominating, and never letting go. Just as I intend to do with his.

EPILOGUE
SIXTEEN YEARS LATER

CALIX

There's something to be said about walking into your own home. One you feel inspired, loved, and challenged by the family you've surrounded yourself with inside said home. My ol'lady is sitting at the table, finishing up homework with our fifteen-year-old daughter, Linden. Our son, Racer, is barely nine and fussing with his brother about some video game they're playing. Kyan is clearly losing. He might be four years older than Racer, but those two normally get along great.

Linden stretches her arms above her head at the same time Ten's eyes meet mine. Stalking over, I lean down and place a kiss on my ol'lady's mouth. Or I might also say my wife's mouth since she's been that too for almost sixteen years. I knew Big Oaks didn't have much time left on this earth so when we hit three months together with the same intensity as day one, I asked for her hand.

Thank fuck Big Oaks, that old hardass fucker, was tough enough to last almost a year after that. He saw Linden being born, his first grandchild…before he died two months later. That was a hard as fuck time for all of us. One of the things that pulled us through was that the club, mine as well as Zack's, were all showing so much support. That's when brotherhood, trust, respect, and friendship shine through.

I had the honor of taking her on a ten-day vacation two months after that. I planned the whole thing to make her relax and able to let herself go to focus on the future. We both needed it. Beach, sunshine, sipping weird fruity cocktails while getting sand in our butts. We both came back stronger and dammit…we manage to love one another a tiny bit more every day since then. Just imagine how big ass our love for one another is right in this moment in time. Bigger than this fucking universe, that's for fucking sure.

"I left C.Rash and his ol'lady in charge of the last details for the barbeque for tomorrow," I tell Ten.

"How many are coming over?" Ten questions.

The corner of my mouth twitches and I let my eyes wander to Linden before I answer. "Almost all of them, including kids."

Linden's eyes light up and I have to keep my laughter at bay when I hear Ten's worried sigh. Oh, yeah. I didn't just give up a chapter when I transferred to this one. We're still in close contact. Not only that but seeing everyone had kids…well, Zack and Blue had twins. Twice. You might say our kids have also settled friendships. Or crushes, whatever, that's for those youngsters to find out and to be honest…it's funny as fuck. Even more when the teenagers are showing off or get into a fight.

"Is it okay if I make some cookies?" Linden asks Ten.

"Sure," Ten says while Kyan and Racer jump up, asking if they can help out.

And yeah, my sons both love to bake and do the kind of stuff daughters do too because I'm not like my father. I don't believe in his kind of upbringing. And the way Ten was raised as a daughter of a Prez shows how fierce and strong she turned out. That's the kind of thing I want for my kids, all of them. To let them be themselves without forcing them into a direction that's implied on us by our ancestors. Fuck that.

"Just be careful, kids. And remember those things are hot when they come out of the oven." I chuckle, because every damn time someone forgets and shoves a cookie into their mouth the second they're out of the oven.

"I'll take number two," Ten murmurs.

See? What did I tell you? "Fine, I'll take number one."

I can't help but chuckle because it's come to the point where we take bets on who burns their mouth with a hot cookie first.

Ten stands up and slides her arms around me. Holding each other close, we watch how our kids start to take over the kitchen. Yeah, we're one tight family in the club, with other chapters, but the one that fills my heart the most is the one I'm surrounded by now. My woman in my arms, our kids taking pleasure in the little things in life.

I intend to grab and hold on to the best things life has to offer. And switching chapters all those years ago was the best damn thing that ever happened to me.

SIX YEARS AFTER THAT...

"It's like watching a swan dance." Blue chuckles.

Ten groans. "That's not funny and it's all your fault. Why did you have to pop out twins? Your boys are giving our daughter hell."

"Aw, Tenley, don't worry so much. Our girls are strong and can hold their own," C.Rash's ol'lady chimes in.

Tenley turns to me. "Maybe we should rethink these monthly barbecue parties with both chapters?"

I turn to Zack and that fucker has a huge grin on his face. "No can do, Tenley. Us Prez's need to have these face to face discussions and since our chapters have grown close over time...hell, some brothers have jumped from one to the other so we're all one big happy family. Us meeting like this can't stop."

"Don't talk about a big family," Blue squeaks. "I had twins, twice. Our boys are ol'lady hunting and our girls are throwing looks at Feargal's sons. Dammit, what if they hook up? We need laws. No dating until they're forty. Yes. That sounds good."

"I second that." Ten nods.

"Oh, I don't know," Nerd interrupts. "Our girl looks so sweet in the arms of Deeds and Lips' son. I was against it at first, another damn MC...scary as hell, but you know what? Those bikers were brought up with the kind of values we respect and would want for our children. It could be worse...like Lips' daughter running off with,"

"Nooooo, we shall not speak of that incident again." Tenley slaps a hand over Nerd's mouth.

"Yeah, that was a war both our chapters barely survived. Fucking Lost Valkyries MC. We should have handled that differently." I sigh, remembering the head to head that mess brought us.

"That's the burden we carry, right Prez? Hence the reason we meet regularly to talk shit through and back each other up," Zack tells me.

"Ain't that the truth." I smack him on the back.

I've never had a vision in mind to become a Prez yet it was the best thing that ever happened to me. Well, second best because first place goes to my wife and children. I'm proud as fuck about all of them.

Standing strong behind me with all the screwed-up moments and dilemmas our life and this club has faced. Yet we're as strong as ever. The tie between chapters has strengthened through the years. It already was from the start, since Zack has been my Prez for years. Though when you've been friends, have a group of ol'ladies who all get along, have kids that grow up together all around the same age...that shit grows an even tighter bond.

So here we stand. Old fuckers keeping an eye on the youth that's going to be the future of Areion Fury MC. Who the fuck cares if they're Ohio, Illinois, Rockford, or whatever. As long as they carry on the Areion Fury legacy. One we as Prez, VP, and brothers worked and fought hard for.

With the dance in front of us, heated glances from young brothers checking out their future ol'lady... yeah...not one fragment of worry tainting the air around us. That's the future right there, allowing us to revive the good old days. Putting our feet up and enjoy a quiet retirement.

"Aw, fuck. Your son did not just punch mine," Dams growls at C.Rash.

"Pretty sure ours is now heading for yours, Blue. Dammit, great comeback though. Shit. Shouldn't you guys interfere or something?" Ten eyes me and Zack.

I grab my beer and sit down. "I'm gonna pass. VP... you should handle it."

C.Rash groans. "If I get hit in the fucking eye again, I'm taking your private jet for a week in the Bahamas with my ol'lady."

I raise my beer. "Deal."

"Come on, Dams, us VP's gotta stick together," C.Rash states.

"Any chance I get the same deal as C.Rash?" Dams eyes Zack.

"Fuck, no." Zack chuckles. "Then you should have joined their chapter, but instead you're stuck with me and I don't own a damn jet."

"Handle it, Dams!" I snap. "They're about to bump into the bar and that means no more beer. You guys pull the youngsters apart, I'll make sure the jet is fueled up and at your disposal. For the both of you."

Dams grins and jogs off with C.Rash, pulling our kids apart. C.Rash takes a punch in the face by Feargal's son so hard it makes even me wince.

"Damn," Zack mutters from my right.

"You can say that again," I mutter and take a sip from my beer. "You coming over to our place next month?"

Zack grins at my question. "Hell yeah, we'll bring the kids...let's see who gets punched in the face next time. And you owe me fifty bucks. I think it was less than an hour before the first punch was thrown."

"You sure?" I ask. "Because I thought I took the 'within thirty minutes' bet and I even had the brother right who got one in the face."

"I'm taking C.Rash next time. That fucker always gets one in the face. Easy money," Zack states and we both clink our bottles together.

"Shouldn't you two be ashamed of yourselves?" Nerd glares at us along with the other ol'ladies.

"What?" Zack shrugs. "That right there," he points behind the women, at the fight that's now broken up, "is exactly what we did when we were their age and look how we turned out. We've fought harder battles, faced even tougher enemies and each of us still manage to have a damn hot ol'lady, fine kids, amazing brothers and friendships. The past is solid, nothing to change about that…but seeing those youngsters, they are the future. They're not backing down but standing ground. So yeah…from the way I think we turned out and how I'm looking at it? It's pretty damn good, if you ask me." Zack holds out his beer bottle again.

I clink mine against his again. "Pretty damn good, brother," I agree.

THE END

This Areion Fury MC series is complete,
but Areion Fury MC will return with a new series!
With Calix as their Prez, the Ohio Chapter will have
enough bikers who need their story to be told.

"Calix" Areion Fury MC #6

My beta team; Neringa, Tracy, Judy, Tammi,
my pimp team, my bestie Christi, and to you,
as my reader…
Thanks so much! You guys rock!

Contact:

I love hearing from my readers.

Email:

authoresthereschmidt@gmail.com

Or contact my PA **Christi Durbin**

for any questions you might have.

facebook.com/CMDurbin

Visit Esther E. Schmidt online:

Website:

www.esthereschmidt.nl

Facebook - AuthorEstherESchmidt

Twitter - @esthereschmidt

Instagram - @esthereschmidt

Pinterest - @esthereschmidt

Signup for Esther's newsletter:

http://esthereschmidt.nl/newsletter

Join Esther's fan group on Facebook:

https://www.facebook.com/groups/estherselite

MORE BOOKS
BY
ESTHER E. SCHMIDT

MC
LOST VALKYRIES

MARLON

NEON MARKSMAN MC

THE DUDNIK CIRCLE

PEACOCK

THE FAULTS OF OUR SINS

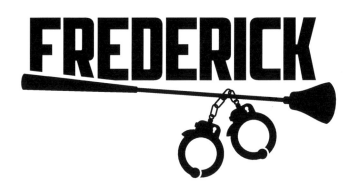

FREDERICK

Swamp heads
SERIES

Manufactured by Amazon.ca
Bolton, ON